SISTER ON TRIAL

Hot-shot surgeon Colum Macadam blamed Shelley Vyner, sister on the Women's Surgical Ward, for the Mack the Knife nickname bestowed on him by her nurses. It was sharpened scalpels at ten paces, until the day Shelley was attacked by an angry drunk. When Macadam came to her rescue she realized he was not such an ogre after all. But then a brilliant surgeon from Macadam's past appeared on the scene—a surgeon who happened to be a beautiful woman. Her appearance convinced Shelley that all she really wanted was to become Colum Macadam's wife.

SISTER ON TRIAL

Valerie Benson

ATLANTIC LARGE PRINT
Chivers Press, Bath, England.
Curley Publishing, Inc.,
South Yarmouth, Mass., USA.

Library of Congress Cataloging-in-Publication Data

Benson, Valerie.
   Sister on trial / Valerie Benson.
      p.   cm.—(Atlantic large print)
   ISBN 0–7927–0803–2 (softcover : lg. print)
   1. Large type books.   I. Title.
[PR6052.E542S57   1992]
823'.914—dc20   91–20607
                                                            CIP

British Library Cataloguing in Publication Data available

This Large Print edition is published by Chivers Press, England, and
Curley Publishing, Inc, U.S.A. 1992

Published by arrangement with Robert Hale Limited

U.K. Hardback ISBN 0 7451 8243 7
U.K. Softback ISBN 0 7451 8255 0
U.S.A. Softback ISBN 0 7927 0803 2

CHAPTER ONE

Shelley Vyner knew she should have stopped this character-bashing the moment it started. But she was too involved herself to stamp immediately on a plain statement of truth. Women's Surgical was overwhelmed with new cases, and it was ninety per cent due to this new surgeon, she fumed.

It was her morning review. All sisters did it, and Women's Surgical was her domain. Her blue book was on her desk, already open, the Bible of her daily work.

Of course, her Staff Nurse, Karen Barnwell, was only putting into words what they all thought. Karen was an agency nurse, and as outspoken as a nest of young blackbirds. Her auburn hair always seemed to have a sparkle of defiance about it, and coupled to the fascinating lights in her russet green eyes gave her a vibrancy that all the young housemen would have liked to stake a claim to.

But she brushed them aside with the ease and casual manner of long experience, unusual in one still only twenty-three.

Shelley liked her enormously, despite Karen's fending off fellow nurses as efficiently as she fended off advances from the male staff. As an agency nurse, she was

1

strictly a nine-to-fiver. And it was a tribute to Karen's skill, patience with her part of the ward, and willingness to take over the work of any of the young students who found themselves wilting under the strain, that she was so popular. Women's Surgical was no place for weaklings, and she could not help the thin smile that sometimes crept unwillingly to her mouth as she recalled what some of the less willing nurses called her. Sister Immaculate. Perfect herself, and unwilling to tolerate slackness in others.

But now it was somebody else being labelled with a name as riveting as her own that brought a warning flash to her usually cool blue eyes as Karen Barnwell concluded her vivid description of the new surgeon who seemed to have no other purpose in life than the cramming into twice as many beds as the ward possessed the successful results of his operations.

And he was successful. Brilliant at his job—if only he would sometimes let a smile lighten the frozen rigidity of his features. Although Shelley was surprised to realise how she could feel such a spark of jealousy when he flashed a sudden smile at one of his patients when he visited them for a post-op survey.

'No wonder they call him Mack the Knife!' Karen's melodiously clear voice belled out. She was speaking with more than her usual frankness. Evidently a reprimand of the day before, when she had done something that had caused Colum Macadam to lower his dark brows at her.

'Like a conveyor-belt!' Karen ended, only to turn with deadly slowness as she became all too aware of a chilling silence.

Shelley felt something wither inside her, but the very firm control she had trained herself to exercise at all times when she was in the ward took over, and she raised a hand.

'Thank you, nurses,' she said in her soft voice that could somehow ring like steel on steel when she was not pleased. 'You may go now.'

Grave-faced, though Shelley knew very well that Joanne Little, her youngest nurse, pert as a robin, but already learning to take a pride in the way she was developing under a sister who was amazingly much kinder than gossips labelled her, was dying to giggle.

Black brows riveted together, Colum Macadam watched the nurses parade past him, then turned the full power of those formidable eyes on Shelley.

'Do you approve of nurses gossiping about their superiors, Sister?' he slammed at her. She could tell he was more than mildly annoyed. There was a tiny muscle at the corner of his strong mouth—she felt a ridiculous flutter in her carefully controlled calm. Could such a granite mouth be tender to kiss? She was startled at the impish thought. She could expect such a whimsy from young Little, but she was the sister who was spoken of in terms of awe by new entrants to the hospital.

'Not at all, sir,' Shelley replied calmly. She had herself firmly in control now, though traces of that impish thought concerning his mouth still lingered. 'In general, my nurses are far too busy to waste time in gossiping. I am sorry you arrived just in time to hear Nurse Barnwell venting her feelings, but if you want the truth, that name is common among all who know you here. It is your own fault you earned it.'

Macadam's mouth was like a trap. He had not expected a mere nurse, even a sister, to be so little in awe of him. It was definitely not in the rule-book. Nurses—all of them—were to be mute in the presence of consultants, unless asked a question, when a simple 'Yes, sir,' or 'No, sir,' would suffice.

He was about to speak, but Shelley moved past him, to close her door firmly. Only too well she knew every eye in the ward was riveted on the two of them. Closing the door would at least cut off the sound from their TV drama. For she felt in the mood for a real up-and-downer. She echoed Karen Barnwell's criticism in every respect.

'You forget yourself, Sister!' Macadam snapped. 'You are impertinent. It is not in

4

the province of a nurse, even one as efficient as I believe you to be, to comment upon the practice of a consultant. You are here to carry out our wishes. And if I choose to end the sufferings of as many patients as I can, it is not up to you to criticise. It is your duty to cope!' His eyes blazed. 'I trust you have heard of our huge waiting list?'

'You forget one thing, Mr Macadam.' Shelley's voice was a silken rapier against the harsh bludgeon of the consultant's temper. 'Whereas you finish your operation in one, two, three or four hours, I and my nurses have to care for those patients as long as perhaps a month or more. We are overwhelmed. There are simply not enough nurses to cope with the patients you insist on throwing us. It is as simple as that. You must slow down.'

She faced him, and the stars in her eyes with which she had entered the profession, knowing it was the only thing she wanted to do, were back again. She was young for a sister, and she realised what a poor opponent she made for a man on his way up, who did not seem to care whose back he planted his Gucci shoes on in his upward progress.

Her words seemed to halt him for a moment, long enough to take a fresh look at this sister whose outspokenness seemed to match that of her nurses.

His height lessened her five foot eight, but

she was still tall enough not to have to tilt her head back too far to look into his stormy grey eyes. And that head, tilted back, seemed to become her so that he only stopped himself in time from drawing in a breath. Nurses had no place in his ambitious schedule, but something about this one gave him pause.

And in that pause, Shelley took clearer note of him. She was already only too familiar with his height and broad shoulders, though she felt herself too old to do any sighing over masculine looks. There were hordes of marvellous young men around now. The better diets and better living of the post-war years were producing remarkable young people.

But now, facing Macadam, she grew aware of an aura of perpetual challenge about him, of a life that had been meeting one hindrance after another. So that challenge was now a need—and if he met it in Women's Surgical, so much the worse for them.

Shelley found her breath come less easily. The harsh dominance about him was too strong for her to ignore. She saw his lips tighten, and realised the scene might go further than she wished, or was good for her or the ward. She had long ago determined never to be ridden over roughshod by any consultant, and though most of them were caring, knowledgeable people, there were still far too many who seemed to think they

6

carried a mantle of supreme authority about them.

A scurry about her closed door forced them both to silence. The door swished open, and Jo Little's flushed face took their attention to a common objective.

'Please, Sister, could you...?'

'Excuse me, sir.' Shelley brushed past Macadam, and walked swiftly in the wake of Nurse Little to where a green curtain had been pulled roughly aside.

Karen Barnwell turned from the bed of the patient as Shelley arrived. Karen was concerned but not flustered as she stood aside for Shelley to make her own examination.

'I think she's bleeding internally,' Karen said quietly, too quietly for the patient to overhear. Shelley nodded, lips compressed. It was altogether too bad for Mrs. Mason. A plump, normally rosy-cheeked housewife, who had come in for a hysterectomy, and was thought to be doing well. She had been uneasy the night before, and Shelley had remained late on the ward to help the SEN and the one student nurse who would have to shoulder the burden of the night hours alone, save for an occasional visit from the night sister. Totally unfair, but that was how it was.

'You had better call for Mr Redfern,' Shelley said quietly. 'Mrs Mason is his patient. 'If you...'

'No use calling for Redfern,' came the voice behind them. Unnoticed, Macadam had insinuated his bulk inside the curtain, and his eyes were professionally on the patient. Mrs Mason was obviously unwell. Damp forehead, fevered cheeks, lips tight in pain.

'I think . . . ' Shelley began, but Macadam brushed her aside, murmuring he'd make his own examination.

Biting her lip, Shelley refused to meet Karen's commiserating glance, and had to concede that Macadam did a superior job of examining Mrs Mason.

'You were quite right, Sister.' Macadam joined her at the sink where they both washed their hands. It seemed to breed a kinship that for one fleeting moment warmed Shelley. She was all business as she listened to the surgeon agreeing with her unfinished speculation that there was internal bleeding. Nothing for it but to have her down in theatre again, as soon as possible.

On her way to the sink, Shelley had whispered to Karen to have the theatre apprised to an urgent case, and already there was a porter on the scene with a trolley.

'Never mind that,' Macadam said sharply, already in charge. 'We'll push her down in her bed. Much better than shifting her on and off a trolley.'

Shelley nodded for Jo Little, for her to go down with the patient, customary for a nurse,

8

and also to hold the drip bottle until it could be attended to in the theatre.

Macadam took hold of the head of the bed, and began pushing. Shelley fell in step with him as they wheeled Mrs Mason out, into the corridor, and towards the lift. 'If Mr Redfern is unavailable, perhaps his registrar could attend to it,' she murmured.

Still pushing, Macadam bent a black brow towards her. 'Indeed, Sister, but I do not think Redfern would relish his assistant tidying up his work. So humiliating, don't you think?'

As Shelley remained silent, the stern look vanished. Was it possible Macadam was laughing at her? 'Connors can assist me,' Macadam said with the certainty of one not to be contradicted. 'And have that young Bennet called. A regular eager beaver. Haunts the theatre. If all goes well, maybe we'll make his day by allowing him to close.'

They were at the lift, and he turned his gaze once more on Shelley. 'Well, Sister, no need for you to wait. Mrs Mason is in good hands. You can have her back shortly.'

He turned to face the lift doors, as if she was no longer an object of his attention.

She had to bite her lip as she walked away. He had been so dismissive. Almost laughing at her anxiety. And she was anxious. Despite her supposed aloofness, she liked to know the background of all her patients. The daughter

9

who had married, and now finding marriage no key to Paradise. She was badly needed to counter her husband's short temper and impatience—mingled perhaps with fright— for Mr Mason was now finding how important a wife was to him.

Back on the ward, it somehow seemed humdrum. Apart from Mrs Mason, everything was going along smoothly. In fact, she had time to treat a couple of patients herself, and instruct Erica Green, her second year, in the treatment of gall-bladder nursing.

Shelley missed the practical nursing she was removed from since her elevation from staff nurse. Now, she was glad the chronic shortage of nurses meant her taking on more and more of the work she thought she had left behind when she attained her sister's blues. There were no longer enough nurses to cope with the patients' everyday needs. Needs all the more urgent now because of Macadam's hectic operations schedule.

It was definitely time something was done, particularly about Macadam. For a few moments there had been a fleeting time of shared intimacy between them in attending to Mrs Mason, but Shelley pushed that aside. Macadam might have relaxed for a minute or two, but tomorrow he would be pushing again, trying to funnel his patients into an already bulging Women's Surgical. And one thing, Shelley was determined she was having no extra beds cluttering up the middle of her ward.

She frowned, one hand resting lightly on the cover of her blue book, already too full of things to do the next day. Perhaps a word with the PNO . . .

But of course, it took time to get in to see the PNO. The SNO would have done if she had been made of sterner stuff. But though a good enough organiser, and adept at dealing with the masses of paper-work that seemed to increase daily, she was little use in trying to impose any authority on the array of consultants who insisted on their way of doing things.

If she had not been so determined in the purpose of her visit, Shelley might have been intimidated by the frosty nod of the PNO's secretary. A newly appointed young woman eagerly stepping up from a lower position in Barding General, who had visions one day of stepping into Rhea Bryce's place.

Mere nurses, even in the blues of a sister, her only too ambitious sniff said, had no business interrupting the clinically arranged day of a principal nursing officer, whose life was more worthily spent in dealing with nobody under the rank of assistant administrator.

Nor did it add to the secretary's day that the insignificant nursing person she ushered into the Holy of Holies was greeted with a

11

sincere smile from Rhea Bryce. And a request for tea.

Tea, indeed! The secretary primmed her lips, far too daunted to mutter in the presence. Tea—for a nurse!

It was habit, rather than to intimate to Shelley that Rhea Bryce's time was limited, that made her glance at her watch. There were so many calls on her, but she was pleasant enough when she lifted her cool grey eyes to Shelley, and nodded as the secretary placed the tea-tray squarely on the large flat desk.

'No phone calls for five minutes, Miss Sims,' Thea Bryce ordered, further increasing Miss Sims' ire. Whatever was her principal thinking of!

'Now, Sister.' Rhea Bryce's smile was as real as the icy glints that could flash past her gold-rimmed spectacles when she was not pleased. 'I am sure you have come for something important.'

Pleasant enough, but still a warning that Shelley had better not be a time-waster.

'About my nurses, Ma'am,' Shelley began, relishing the tea—Earl Grey of course. The PNO had her privileges. 'I am sorry to say my ward is wretchedly understaffed.'

Rhea Bryce's brows were raised. 'Surely, Sister, isn't that a matter for my deputy, the SNO?'

Shelley's lips firmed. She was going to have

12

her say and damn the torpedoes. 'Normally, Ma'am, yes. But this is something I am afraid is beyond her scope. You know, of course, that we have a new surgeon, Colum Macadam?'

'Of course.' The grey eyes softened. 'Good God!' Shelley thought. 'Has that wretched man suborned the PNO with an Irish smile and a dollop of Blarney! I never thought she could be persuaded by anything short of a Cruise missile!'

'He seems too be an excellent surgeon,' Shelley went on quickly, knowing her time was almost up, 'but the trouble is, he is far too efficient for my ward to cope. We are inundated with what seems to be nothing less than a torrent of patients fresh from Mr Macadam's scalpel. If I had a full staff, I should be delighted. But with only three nurses, and one of them an agency nurse whose day ends sharp at five o'clock, I just do not have the trained staff to deal with so many dressings, treatments and chart-fillings. And Mr Macadam insists on every chart being rigorously and fully kept.'

'You mean you expect me to tell—rather, ask—a consultant surgeon to stop working so hard? You really expect me to remonstrate like that?'

'Damn protocol!' Shelley thought riotously. 'I'm not having my nurses worked down to their ankles if I can help it!'

13

Aloud, she said calmly, 'Yes, Ma'am, I do. It is no longer a case of pulling our fingers out. Last week,' she went on grimly, determined to let it all hang out, 'on nights, we had to make do with only two student nurses. First years. The week before, I had to spend three hours of my time off every night helping the night staff because we had some very exhausting cases. It just cannot go on. Even now I have to keep persuading this agency nurse to stay. She is an excellent nurse, even though she does insist on stopping work religiously at her appointed time. She can get plenty of work at twice the money if she wants to. I have to load a lot of extra work on to her because my other staff nurse is away ill for goodness knows how long. My other nurses are still only students.'

She got to her feet. There was no need to tell Rhea Bryce that at the end of their training, a full third of nurses left the profession. Too little money, too much work, too unsocial hours. It was a constant drain that was making the lives of all conscientious nurses an uphill battle.

'I am sure I can leave it in your hands, Ma'am.'

'Yes, thank you, Sister.' It was obvious her next appointment was on the PNO's mind. But her frosty look left no doubt she would see to things.

Somehow, Shelley got herself out, and past

the even more chilly secretary, already on her feet with a stiffly held pad.

Back on her ward, Shelley would have forgotten about her visit to the PNO, but for the news given her by a grim-faced Karen Barnwell. The agency staffer looked ready to throw bedpans in a thundering cascade down the ward.

She marched into Shelley's office, half a step behind, her heels stamping on to the floor as if something had to be hurt.

'We've had an extra admission forced on us,' she huffed, battle cries in her russet-coloured eyes. 'A gall bladder.'

'Gall bladder! Extra!' Shelley felt out of it. 'But we were already prepared for a gall bladder. Mrs Ketchum.'

'Ah, but our beamish boy, Mack the Knife, was in here last night with a special he drummed up from nowhere. Insisted it must be added to today's list. Saw to the woman's prepping and everything. Made an early start and was halfway through before you'd even made your morning porridge.'

'But how could that happen?' Shelley whispered, as if to herself. 'I did not know a thing about it.'

'Oh, Macadam arranged everything about nine o'clock last night. Got the two student nurses to co-operate, moved one of our almost ready-to-go-home cases to a vacant bed in Women's Medical, and shifted things a bit more so his new case could go into one of our side rooms. Seems this new patient is a friend of a friend,' she ended bitterly, resenting the way consultants could manipulate their lists so that friends of friends could jump the queue.

'Oh, did he!' Shelley's mood was blacker than her hair. It was bad enough Macadam pushing too many of his cases into the ward—some of his fellow surgeons were already beginning to mutter—but to have him interfere with her ward arrangements, really, it could not go on. Consultants were already treated with far too much consideration for their self-ascribed godlike qualities, but this was too much altogether!

Simmering, she could not be expected to forget this new intrusion. Not that it hindered her giving the extra patient full attention when she finally arrived. She was a private patient, and Macadam would see that she was given every attention.

And it was as she was standing by the bed of this Mrs Allday, waiting for her finally to struggle out of her doped state, that she was found by a tight-lipped Macadam.

'A word with you, Sister, if you please.' Macadam stood in the doorway of the side ward where Mrs Allday had been put. He filled it, and if his figure had not done so, the blackness of his temper would have done it.

'In your office,' he said tightly.

16

Shelley turned a cool gaze on him that belied the fury inside her. He was ordering her as if she were a recalcitrant schoolgirl being summoned to the headmaster's office. No sister worthy of her blues would have put up with such discourtesy.

'In a moment, sir,' she said in a voice calm enough, but subtly able to lash him like a whip. 'One of my nurses will bring you a cup of tea while you wait.'

She turned back to Mrs Allday, knowing she did not need to be there, but making damn sure Macadam got the message.

She steeled herself, expecting an explosion. But without another word he turned on his heel, unaware that in his absence she had let out a long-held breath.

★   ★   ★

'Sister!' He was waiting for her, sprawled on the spare chair, dark hair no blacker than his mood, though he stood up politely as she entered the office.

She thanked Karen Barnwell's quick intuition for the tea-tray already there, and took time to pour herself a cup, to ease her less worked-up self into the fracas she knew was waiting.

'Now, perhaps you will explain why you had the ball-blasting nerve to complain about me to the PNO!' Macadam's voice was low-pitched, but it could have smashed a bronze bell. 'What on earth do you think you were playing at, going up there, whining about what I do! Did it ever enter your stupid little head that I do not need to answer to a nurse, even the sacred Sister Vyner, for permission to do my work? I flayed myself for eleven years to get where I am now, and if you think someone like you is going to dictate to me...!'

For a moment he ran out of words. His gaze locked with Shelley's, and when he found hers did not drop before his fury, he seemed to subside like a great wave lifting against a sturdy rock, and being forced back on itself.

Shelley remained standing. She had to, to keep control of herself. It was no easy thing, to refuse to be intimidated by this man. She could feel his masculine power reaching out to her, by his very presence almost smothering her. Only the rightness of her stand, and the sheer grinding workload this man wanted to thrust on her and her nurses kept her steadfast in front of him.

'If you have eyes, Mr Macadam,' she dropped her words, flintlike, on him, 'you will be able to see my entire staff. One staff nurse, who leaves us remorselessly as the hand of fate every day at five o'clock. She is an agency nurse, with no call to stay behind her fixed time, unlike the rest of my staff who

18

have to stay till the work is finished. And count them, Mr Macadam.' Her stress on the 'Mister' was like a whip. 'Three! Nurse Green, that slim blonde by Mrs Gannon's bed. A second year. Nurse Little ... ' Her tilted head indicated the elfin girl with dimpled cheeks helping a woman down the ward to make her first obligatory steps. 'And Nurse Rhodes.' Another nod pointed out the plump girl whose cap never would remain at the correct tilt on her head. She had a springy mass of mouselike curls that tended to push her cap all over the place.

She was fumble-fisted, another first year, but wearing her green belt with pride. Some day she would be the prouder wearer of a staff nurse's purple epaulettes and belt, if some overbearing doctor did not first destroy her willingness by peremptory treatment. Shelley had seen that happen more than once, and was determined not to let it happen to any of her staff.

'And just those to cope with thirty patients who have to be attended to throughout the working-day. Medical patients can be left alone, save for charts and drug rounds. But these patients must be overlooked constantly. Drainages to be tended, bandages inspected, and always suspected bleeding to be looked for.'

Out of breath she had to pause. But she felt her heart drop when she found no relaxing in

19

that stiff face confronting her like an enemy.

'Then I recommend, that you, Sister, emerge more frequently from your ivory tower here, roll up your sleeves, and tackle some of the scut work yourself. Get yourself into the work role. Or find something easier, like nursery work. While there is a long waiting-list outside these walls, I am going to work my head off—along with you and your staff!'

CHAPTER TWO

Mercifully, Shelley did not see Macadam all the next day. In moments of less than complete dedication to her mass of paper work, she felt relieved, knowing she could not have been long in his presence without showing her anger. And yet, somewhere in her lingered a sense of disappointment. As if she had been expecting something, and it had not materialised.

She shrugged. Good heavens, she castigated herself. She was a long way from feeling let down because a special male did not appear. It was ten years since she had been through the harrowing experience with Chris Saunders. Chris—even now, she felt a slight frisson of excitement when she recalled him. The wide-shouldered figure, the face too handsome for any everyday male, and the smile that could coax a bird of paradise from any tree anywhere. Sheer magic was the word for it—and it concealed a great big nothing.

Chris was just facade. Beautiful to look at, skilled in all the arts of male domination over woman, and useless in the more subtle ways of keeping a woman satisfied beyond the mere physical. There was always a time you had to get out of bed, Shelley told herself, her face regretful. And in the ordinary day-to-day trivialities, which was really all that life was about, Chris lacked everything needed. He had to live on the peaks, and there were never any left after the first three months. Then he was off to prospect fresh peaks, with a careless, hey nonny no for the peak he was deserting.

Which made it extremely galling for Shelley to realise that Macadam was the first man since Chris really to stir the tiny nerves along her spine. And coupled to that wretchedly off-putting manner of his, that made him the most unwelcome male of males good and bad.

And the knowledge that it was Macadam who was causing this quite unwelcome provocation of all the senses that made a woman a woman caused her to inject an unintended touch of ice into her replies to Mr Goldstein's account of just what he wanted her to look out for in his latest operation.

Chubby as an ideal Father Christmas, though with black curly hair that even threatened to curl its way up from his immaculate white collar towards the square chin on which twice daily shaving could do no more than keep a permanent blueness at bay.

Ben Goldstein surveyed Shelley through his gold-rimmed glasses. Fatherly, for he took a great deal of interest in her, knowing she was the one person he could depend on to watch the patients he entrusted to her ward with the degree of vigilance he expected.

'So—there are nothing but clouds in the sky today, Sister?' he ventured benignly. He was never one to lack curiosity concerning his favourite nurse.

'I'm sorry, sir.' Shelley took a hold on herself. This would never do. Least of all with Goldstein, who was as much her favourite surgeon as she was his nurse. 'I had something on my mind.'

'Don't we all?' chuckled the surgeon. Patiently, out of earshot of his patient, Mrs Carey, he went again through the things he wanted Shelley to watch out for.

'Such a pity.' He rubbed his chubby hands together, more like bladders with chipolatas attached, Shelley thought, knowing that in spite of their apparent clumsiness Goldstein was diabolically clever. Friends boasted he could operate on a humming bird.

'Forty years old,' he said, his voice thick

with gloom and pity. 'And none of it necessary. If she had only been examined sooner. This government...!' He muttered scurrilities against all authority. 'All governments!' he ended, in a grumbling thunder, because he had no politics, and all governments were slack-handed in funnelling money where it was most needed.

'Will she recover?' Shelley asked, knowing it was entirely the wrong thing to ask. But Goldstein did not believe in shirking the issue.

'A good chance. No more.' He patted her on the shoulder. 'We will do our best. And you, my lovely girl, will do all you can do keep up her spirits. In cases of cancer, I always think a determined attitude to getting well is half the battle. That is why we get remissions, remissions which overjoy everybody.'

When he was gone, shuffling along in that bear-like half-trot that horrified his fellow consultants, who could never accustom themselves with their background of the right schools and right medical approach to this big man with his history of thrusting himself up the ladder by sheer gall and ability.

Shelley whisked back the curtains that had given them privacy. She hated curtains drawn round a bed. They always seemed to her to point to something serious.

The increased light round the bed seemed

to cheer up the patient, for Mrs Carey gave her a wan smile.

She had once been good-looking, but though the bones were still there, the high cheekbones that gave Linda Evans and Angie Dickinson their peculiar appeal, the flesh round them was beginning to lose tone and firmness. Lines that should have waited another five or ten years were there in too many stress places. But it was a familiar sight to Shelley. Women who came from poorer families all too often showed much too soon the strain of living and coping with too little money.

'Well, Mrs Carey,' Shelley said, not too brightly, and careful to avoid that nonsense of how-are-we hospitals are so ready to use. It could irritate a sickly-feeling patient beyond endurance when a bright-eyed nurse, obviously in the best of health, tried to couple herself to somebody feeling like an escapee from Hell.

Shelley automatically straightened things on the top of the locker, then took Mrs Carey's wrist in her cool fingers. She often did that to patients, even though her nurses attended to the regular pulses and temperatures. It gave reassurance, and enabled her to keep herself more in touch with how her patients were. Caring human contact was important.

'Do you feel better now you've had a word

with Mr Goldstein?' she went on.

'A little bit,' Mrs Carey said cautiously. Shyly, she seemed subdued, Shelley thought, especially with her husband, who was a burly man from a local car factory, who seemed able to lift whole cars on his own.

'He's very nice, isn't he?'

'He's like that,' Shelley said warmly. 'And do you know what?' she patted the woman lightly on the wrist, 'when he's pleased with how one of his patients does, he always gives them a red rose when they leave.'

A few more words, all calculated to take Mrs Carey's mind off the gravity of her case, and she moved on. Patients could be terribly jealous if she spent too much time on some, and neglected others. Every one had to have her own smile and special word from Sister Shelley. She often thought that public relations did as much good as the surgeons' efforts.

On the way back to her office, where the phone was ringing, she scooped up Nurse Green, whose blonde hair looked silver gilt in the sunshine that speared in through the ward's tall windows. 'You can help me with Mrs Johnson,' Shelley told her, pretending not to notice Nurse Green's slight frown. Colostomies were nobody's special favourite, although all the nurses took extra pains to let the patient feel no distaste applied to treating them.

25

The phone call disposed of, Shelley ushered Nurse Green to the bed two places from the door where Mrs Johnson was waiting for them with a lack of joy that was apparent in her subdued reply to Shelley's greeting.

Curtains drawn, Shelley took a packet of disposable bags to show both Mrs Johnson and Nurse Green how convenient they were, once their use was accepted.

'It'll be no more nuisance than diabetes, once you get used to it,' Shelley announced firmly. 'A nuisance, but supportable.'

Thin relief took some of the anxieties from Mrs Johnson's face as Nurse Green put away the disposable bags, and took time to settle the woman more comfortably.

'Mr Goldstein will do you tomorrow,' Shelley said soothingly, trying to lessen the impact of the actual operation. 'In the meantime, you can read this little booklet. When you go home, you will have to follow a diet, to make things easier for yourself. It will be quite practical, just a matter of eating the right foods.'

'Gosh, Sister!' Nurse Green said feelingly, as she followed Shelley back to her office. 'You made it all seem nothing much worse than a broken leg.' She shivered theatrically. 'I'd hate it to happen to me!'

'What happen?' Karen Barnwell's cheerful voice caught up with them. She had brought

26

Shelley's tea for morning break—usually
filled with more paper work. It was the only
way to get things done.

'A colostomy!' Nurse Green's eyes were
rounded. 'Gosh!'

'Me, too!' Karen shuddered. Only to nod
her head in comic guilt when Shelley drily
asked them would they prefer Mrs Johnson to
have John Wayne's Big C to the complaint
that filled them with such distaste.

Shelley watched them walk swiftly down
the ward, in a hurry to get their own tea.
Patients had been served. That was one more
thing Karen was so adept at doing, specially
with the niggly patients who kicked up when
their tea was not rightly sugared.

*   *   *

Shelley thought she was lucky to have Karen.
Even though so strict with her hours, she
more than earned her money. She was very
close-mouthed about herself, and Shelley
guessed her home life was very closely
patterned. A child perhaps, looked after by
somebody else all day. Karen wore no ring,
but she was a strong personality, who would
do what she wanted, regardless. Shelley
wished she had another nurse as good. At
least, that would have ensured she would not
be late getting off duty three nights in a row,
she thought tiredly, as she keyed open the

door to her flat.

Once inside, she cheered up, feeling the unostentatious comfort of the place. She had a living-room, bedroom, and small kitchen, in addition to a small bathroom on the first floor of an old house on the fringe of a park. Tall trees made a pleasing view from her bedroom window in the mornings, almost making her forget the dinginess of the paths through the greenery so much frequented by the wrong sort of people at night.

She switched on her kettle. Tea first, then she could sit back for half an hour, feet on a stool while deciding whether to eat out or fix something from her small fridge. Then she frowned. She had forgotten it was Tuesday, when she spent an evening at a battered wives' refuge.

An old schoolfriend, a militant feminist, had started the place, and perhaps unfortunately for Shelley decided her friend was the very person to appear regularly, to do small first aid to the wives' hurts. Shelley often thought a sympathetic ear did more good than balm on bruised faces.

It was a nuisance tonight. She did not feel like going to such a haunt of misery, but her conscience would not allow her to phone Millicent Gilroy with an excuse. Millicent was magnificently healthy, and would have scorned talk of a headache.

'I'll have to stop going there,' Shelley told

herself, beginning to stir. It was just too much, after the stress of the ward, to get immersed in another load of misery. She needed some respite, and she had to laugh, although not altogether joyously, to think of being escorted somewhere splendid by a marvellous young man. Perhaps dinner at the Arlington, in their penthouse restaurant. Opened only a few months previously, the hotel was the spot for the smart set for fifty miles around. The restaurant was perfect for everything Shelley could fantasise about a night out. She had heard about the resident piano player, whose softly rhythmic background would have shaken Fats Waller out of his shoes.

But who would take Shelley Vyner there? She might be a name to think about at Barding General, but among the clientele of the Arlington she would be regarded most likely as a fish out of water. Why, she did not even own so much as a skirt good enough for that squishy penthouse—although, sticking up for herself almost indignantly, she had legs as good as any others to be found there.

It took her a moment to realise it was her buzzer sounding. At the insistence of the two old ladies, one-time schoolmistresses, and still looking the part with many a qualified but approving look at Shelley when they met in the hall, the entrance door to the three-storey house had been fitted with stout locks and a buzzer to alert each apartment.

'We can't trust anybody these days, my dear,' Fanny Wardle, the elder of the two ladies, pointed out severely to Shelley. 'We just can't have any no goods roaming into the place. The landlord will pay half the cost, if we agree to defray the rest. So...'

'Of course.' Shelley agreed gladly. 'I suppose Mr Brogan...'

'He will, my dear,' was the quick response concerning the other tenant. 'He was most willing. Frankly, he admitted he had a physique unable to cope with today's villains.'

So it was settled, and now the small panel on the outer door operated a triple-buzzer system, with a voice announcer. And her buzzer was going, and somebody—heaven knew who—was waiting impatiently for her to answer.

'Yes?' Shelley asked crisply.

'Sister?' That was all, but she could feel the skin on the back of her neck crimping. There would never be a time when she did not recognise that sword-edged voice immediately.

'Mr Macadam!' she exclaimed, almost surprised out of the shoes that she had slipped on out of habit as she crossed the room.

'Do you think you could let me in? I am unarmed, full of only the purest intentions.'

The drawling voice, and the tone of it,

30

giving her an immediate impression of the chiselled face set in an expression of cool disenchantment made Shelley's fingers curl. She was about to tell him to go away, there was not a thing in the world they had to talk about. If he had to speak to her, tomorrow was time enough. For this week, she had just about had her lot with Colum Macadam, damned man! Should have gone in for making roads, like his long dead namesake, instead of turning his talents to cutting people, and not only with a scalpel.

She could sense him waiting there, and it gave her a little malicious pleasure to have it so. Maybe some of that cool derision he had for others which he so often displayed would be fading.

Somehow, without her willing it, her hand reached out for the door release. 'You can come up,' she announced coolly. 'First floor.'

She dropped her hand, and took a step back in dismay. God, what on earth was wrong with her! She didn't want to talk to the damned man! He had bruised her feelings enough for the day—and all at once she was bitingly hungry. Even for one of those ready-in-a-jiff packets from Marks.

She opened the door, and he was there. Seeming to fill the room before he was even in it. She hated to admit it, but the damned man had presence. And knew it!

There he was, still in the doorway, his eyes

31

first on her, then going round the room as if wondering whether it was good enough for him.

And more irritating still, curious about her, her way of life. Did he expect to find a live-in man here? Was that why he had come?

'Oh, come in!' she snapped. 'I can't stand people who hover!'

She motioned him to a chair. Whatever had he come for? She could think of no reason why he should have gone to the trouble of getting her address from records, then coming here when he could have been out with some wonderful blonde—did he prefer blondes, like so many men, the gypsy thought flitted through her mind.

'Well?' she asked, nettled. Was he struck dumb, now he had been admitted, or just trying to unsettle her for some nasty reason of his own? And him all dressed up in a west-country blue worsted that never came off a handy rack, and her still in her rumpled hospital blues. She could have killed him. It was as if he had deliberately sought to put her at a disadvantage.

Colour crept up her cheeks as he remained silent, merely looking at her intently. Did she have a smut on her face, a spot from that gentian violet stain she was always so careful to use, she wondered, going pinker still. Good God, she was a fully experienced sister, not a stupid fifteen-year-old.

'Was there something? Something I forgot to do for one of your cases?' she rushed on, knowing she should have remained the imperturbable Sister Vyner, of Women's Surgical, not gone on babbling like that thing in Alfred Lord Tennyson they'd had to learn in school.

She could not know he was looking at her as something quite different from the capable sister from Barding General. He was looking at her as a woman looking as lovely as she would ever look. A face clean cut in precisely the way a truly gifted painter would have relished. Eyes the blue sometimes seen when the sun strikes at just the right angle on an Irish lough. And lips...

He wrenched himself out of thoughts that seemed totally out of place at that moment. All at once, Sister Vyner was back in her hospital mode, stiff-backed and equally stiff-necked, fighting off invaders to her spotlessly run ward.

'Would you like a cup of tea?' she offered stiffly. Damn him, whatever had brought him here! But at least, there was still tea in the pot, and she had originated in Liverpool, where a visitor to the house was offered tea as soon as they set foot in the door.

'No sugar.' He smiled his acceptance, dwarfing the cup with his hand. Leaned back a little, still regarding her. By heavens, she was some girl! Here, in her own place, she

33

seemed to have shed five or six years from the strict disciplinarian of Women's Surgical.

'I've come to offer you an apology,' he offered surprisingly. 'I was much too abrasive yesterday. I'm sorry.'

Taken aback, Shelley sat up straighter. Surely this Macadam bod was of the 'Never apologise, never explain' school. Yet here he was, not abject as a schoolboy certainly, but without that bulldozer set to his jaw.

'Well . . . ' She shrugged, not yet ready to be mollified. 'You have to understand that nurses have problems, especially nowadays. There are just not enough of us to cope with the demands on us.'

Her eyes did a damned good job of boring into him, he conceded. Pretty eyes, too.

'The after-care of patients, with you doctors introducing new techniques all the time, giving us fresh problems, is more important than ever. And you don't seem to realise, never look at it from our point of view. You stand back from the table, snap out "Close up!" to your assistant, and you think that's it. Nothing else to worry about. That is just when a nurse's work begins. And it is work. Highly skilled work, and people like me are having to put up with more and more unskilled workers. Nurses barely out of PTS are expected to cope like an SRN. It is getting worse, and something must be done about it!'

34

Unconsciously, Macadam leaned back, half-drunk tea forgotten. There was a fire in this girl that matched the fire he knew he himself possessed. And it stirred something in him. Something he had thought no girl at Barding ever would do. Nurses were part of his professional world, but he had never reckoned any of them would matter to him personally. Now, was this something his carefully laid plans had never reckoned with?

He thought again of the thick indignation on Ben Goldstein's face when he unloaded on him what he thought about sisters who took too much on themselves.

'The cheek of it!' Macadam had fumed. 'Going to the PNO and complaining about a consultant.'

'Time you got yourself modernised,' Goldstein told him without sympathy. 'Things are not like they used to be, when the tread of a consultant down the ward shook the earth. You can call the nursing profession a sleeping giant ready to wake up and roar any time now.

'Us lot,' and he grinned his face-wide grin that captivated everybody, 'are not as important as we once were. Nobody quakes in their ward shoes any more. Mere porters can start strikes and pick and choose who comes through the hospital gates. All sorts of odds and sods are deciding they are not going to put up with our lordly ways any longer.

Let me tell you, our good Shelley Vyner, our angel of mercy in Women's Surgical, will bend over backwards to accommodate us surgeons, even the awkwardest, and believe me, there are some right sods in our profession. Let me tell you about her.'

He put a hand on Macadam's shoulder, and squeezed, and his hand could have crushed stone.

'Two months after our Shelley was made sister, I developed flu. You know the feeling? Like being hit on the head with a loaded furniture van. If somebody up and shot you you would thank them for evermore. Our Shelley heard about it, that I lived all alone in a flat, and round she came. Bottle of whisky in one hand, scrubbing-brush in the other. She came round four nights in succession, cleaned the place up so you could do a heart-and-lung in it, cleaned me up well enough to do it, and fed me. Now if you don't go right round and beg her pardon, I will personally hit you so hard your nose will dribble down the back of your neck.'

Macadam came to himself, realising Shelley was looking at him strangely. 'Well, I've apologised, dressed myself in sackcloth and ashes, so now—will you have dinner with me?'

The invitation spilled out in a rush, as if he was not in the habit of tendering such to girls he hardly knew.

36

'Dinner...!' Shelley went rigid. Dinner! Exactly what she had been fantasising about, when she was considering warming up one of those Marks packages she was using so much lately. With all the elegant fixings? He did not look the type to hold a tray in MacDonalds. Not in that suit.

She savoured the offer, thinking how uplifting it would feel and look to walk ahead of him into some prestigious cocktail lounge, with a bowing maître d' to do the honours, then dinner—and she was hungry. It was on her lips to accept, and to blazes with any injured feelings—when the thought came to her.

She couldn't. Not tonight. Not Tuesday.

'I'm sorry, she said stiffly. 'It is out of the question. I have a previous appointment.'

He stared. Not exactly shocked, but surprised. He did not offer too many dinner invitations, for without being any Narcissus he knew no girl would ever refuse. Not him!

'Your boyfriend?' he asked, mouth twisting a little.

'That is none of your business,' she told him flatly.

He sat up straighter. He wanted her to accept now more than when the stray thought had come to him. The perfect olive-branch. She was no subservient moppet. She was beautiful. And he would enjoy another battle of words with her. Anything to make those

37

lovely eyes flash, and that enchanting head tilt back on that perfect neck as if she were ready to repel all boarders.

'No, I'm sorry, it isn't. I just thought, as a peace offering...'

'We'll be at peace as long as you understand my position,' Shelley said firmly. 'But I really do have another appointment.'

It was on the tip of her tongue to angle, to say 'Perhaps another time,' but damn him, she wasn't going to let him see she thought he was something special, once you got behind that forbidding facade.

He spread his hands. Was at the door, when a thought seemed to strike him. Good God, he looked actually sheepish! 'There was one thing, Sister. Dammit, Shelley! I asked you out to dinner, so that gives me a right, doesn't it? Even if you refused, I'm Colum.'

'I know.' Shelley thought it nice to yield a little, and he did look so wonderful. 'But perhaps we had better keep to Mr Macadam, until we get to know each other better.'

She stopped, appalled. It looked as if she were giving him the perfect come-on. Playing a little hard to get. And she hated subterfuge.

'There was one other thing,' Macadam said, fumbling with the door behind him. 'I need a bed for tomorrow. For a patient,' he added hastily, as if afraid to let her think he was propositioning her. 'An emergency.' His brows furrowed his forehead. 'A girl. Twenty years old.' He would have explained further, but she waved him to silence.

'You never give up, do you?' she said, despondent all at once.

He looked away. 'I have to do the best I can, the only way I know I can.'

Shelley shrugged. So much for the apology, the dinner invitation. All so he could wangle another case into the ward. He must think her a pint to the quart.

'Very well, Mr Macadam,' she said frigidly. 'Somehow I'll find you a bed. But don't think this can go on. If I let you have your way like this every time, there'll soon be no room for any cases from the other surgeons. Just this once.'

She was glad he could not see the way her lips drooped as she turned her face away. She had had the last word with a man noted for his irritable intractability—so why wasn't she happy?

CHAPTER THREE

Ordinarily, Shelley perked up when she was going to meet her old schoolfriend, Millicent Gilroy, despite her running the battered wives' refuge she had opened in a large, sadly run-down mansion on the fringe of town. It had once been a very select neighbourhood of produce-merchants, heads of large firms, and professional men. Millicent had retained a sharp-edged sense of humour that found outlet in occasional outbursts as bawdy as a brothel-creeper.

But this evening, Shelley felt depressed. She had to admit she had not enjoyed the last skirmish with Macadam. In spite of the fact that she admired his skill as a surgeon. It was just that at this time in her life she felt she needed someone more responsive to the need she had for a man to comfort her. She had had her share of confrontations. Perhaps it was time to lower her standards slightly, let some man get closer to her, even if she had to overlook some faults.

'Nobody's that perfect!' had been flung at her more than once when she had made it clear that the particular man trying to bring about a closer relationship was not exactly what she had in mind. Especially as...

Then she did smile. Had to suppress a laugh. Gosh, how some men were dashed when they were faced with the outspokenness they loved to dish out to women. They never seemed to grow up, except in their grosser appetites.

'Ha! I'm glad to see somebody feels happy!' Milly Gilroy greeted Shelley with a hug. She was a large, angular woman with little time now for the softer side. Made of steel, she did not boast, rather congratulated herself on more than one occasion, when Shelley had noticed how well she stood up to the misfortunes of her battered guests.

'I was just thinking about men,' Shelley murmured, putting her coat into the large hall wardrobe that one of the inmates had painted a pleasing shade of green-tinged white. Milly saw to it that those of her wives without children with them did things about the place. Even teaching them to fix plugs, clear blocked sinks, anything that cropped up at the refuge.

'Oh, men!' Milly's scornful laugh was expressive. Her experience with the man she had married years ago, in a tempestuous infatuation that all too soon turned sour, had disenchanted her completely.

'Sheer vicious sadism,' Milly had explained to Shelley, a year after the marriage had ended in separation, then divorce. 'He liked to hit people. Women, naturally. He could punch them without fear of getting his wonderful looks impaired. Or so he thought.'

Her grey eyes grew reminiscent, but there was bitterness in her voice when she went on. 'He'd started, just in a temper, now and then. Soon, it got to be a regular thing. When his little world struck a snag, he'd take it home to the little woman. Claimed she liked to be knocked about—God, how these macho brutes kid themselves! A black eye made her properly submissive—and sexy! After all, if

41

she were in a harem she'd be whipped good and proper by one of the eunuchs.'

A pause. 'Then one day, I looked in a mirror, really looked. Can you imagine what it feels like when you see a sunset where your right eye should be? A stormy sunset. And a split in your lip that screamed every time you drank hot tea.

'So the next time I was ready. It was just a playful punch, by his standards, a warning, like, to make me jump about a bit quicker. But I'd been nursing a little brass ornament in my hand all evening, knowing I was going to use it. I just cramped my hand around it, and slugged him right on his beautiful nose.

'My sainted aunt! For a minute there I was appalled. You never saw such blood. I thought he was going to shed the entire twenty pints or whatever it is we carry around inside our skins. And the shape! He rushed to the mirror and screamed. His lovely, lovely nose! For a minute he was ready to commit murder. I had dared to lay a finger on him. His obedient little wifey. By then I'd picked up a brass candlestick he liked to keep on the mantelpiece—he loved brass so long as I cleaned it. I swore I'd kill him if he touched me one more time. Anyway, he was too concerned about his nose to delay getting to the hospital.'

She chuckled, let her angular body give way to gusts of laughter. 'By the time he came back, I'd packed and gone. We only had a rented flat. Furnished. All I needed were my clothes—and I didn't have that many. And that's how I got into this business. Not all wives dare to fight back. They'll stand getting half killed, sooner than let the neighbours know they're getting battered.'

'Any new ones?' Shelley asked, for it was the new ones who generally needed her services. Cuts, bruises, black eyes. Occasional broken arm.

'Just one,' Milly told her. 'Thankfully, the wife-battering season seem to have tapered off. Maybe it's because cricket's taken over from football, and there's not so much aggro going around.'

Shelley found the new woman seeking refuge in the communal lounge. Hardly out of her teens. Shelley suppressed a quick surge of anger, and amaze, at the large black eye the girl was trying to keep turned away from her as if ashamed.

'Sally Vernon,' Milly introduced, a warm arm round the girl's shoulders. 'She's having a little holiday with us. I'm teaching her to cook.'

Milly did those things, Shelley knew. She seemed to take it for granted that wives who came seeking her aid were often short of domestic skills. Maybe that was part of the trouble, Shelley reflected. She acted as a Mother Confessor to most of the women. The very act of Shelley handling their hurt flesh with compassion as well as soothing fingers caused them to unburden themselves.

As did Sally, once Shelley assured herself the girl was not grievously knocked about.

Her husband had been sacked. For what, Sally did not say. The sudden change from affluence, with overlarge hire purchases to pay off, had started it all. Shelley recognised the signs. Less drinking with his mates. No money to spend regardless. It would all lead to permanent disruption unless the girl and her husband could face up the change in their circumstances.

After Shelley finished the few things necessary for her, and listening to another repetition of some life stories, Milly bore her off to her comfortable little sanctum, where she entertained her own friends.

They had finished their tea, and some cakes made by one of the women, when there was a knock on the door, and a head poked round.

Recognition was instant. 'Oh, hello, Mrs Bryan,' Shelley greeted the good-looking woman who gave her a shy, half-smile. 'How are you?'

The woman replied in a few words, almost as if she had forgotten how to express herself freely. She came further into the room to tell Milly she had just come back from a visit to her mother in a nearby town.

'And do you want to come back here,

Phyl?' Milly asked gently. Shelley could see that her friend was examining the woman, looking for signs that all was not well.

'Not for the moment.' The smile was a little freer. 'I've got a little place in Seldon Street. I'm sharing it with a woman I met from work. I've just started a job at Blake's, the motor-spares people.'

'And Harry?'

'For the time being, we'll stay apart,' Phyl Bryan said firmly. 'We've been to marriage counsellors, but Harry thinks all he has to do is promise to be better, and I'll come flying back. But not this time.'

A few more minutes' chat, and Mrs Bryan said she had to leave. She had only come to let Milly know what she was doing, so there would be room for one more to help.

Shelley left with her. They stood together at the end of the short drive to the mansion, between two sandstone pillars that had once supported two ornamental lions but now only misshapen pieces of stone, weathered and worn to nubs.

'You feel quite all right now?' Shelley asked Mrs Bryan. She remembered the woman well from her stay in Women's Surgical a month before. A broken rib—her husband's work—had pierced her lung, and an emergency operation brought her under Shelley's care. It was just after Macadam had come to the hospital, before Shelley had time to know what a hard line he took where his wants were concerned.

'Yes, thank you, Sister,' Mrs Bryan said. 'I'm settling down to a nice way of living. We get on well, the woman I share the place with. She's a widow, so there's no man to trouble either of us.'

The smile vanished from her face. Shelley stared as the woman seemed to wither, and found her arm tightly gripped as Mrs Bryan shrank behind her.

Coming towards them, the man with his head thrust forward like a bull looking for a gate to crash through caught sight of Mrs Bryan, and let out a muffled roar. His steps quickened, and he was half running when he reached them.

'Well, I've found you at last, have I?' he greeted his wife. 'I've been trying to get hold of you for a week. Where the hell have you been?'

'I've been visiting Mother,' Mrs Bryan said. She moved back a step to evade his clutching hand. It was a large hand, and all at once, Shelley was aware of how close he was, and how very angry.

She pushed Mrs Bryan back against the sandstone pillar, and faced the man. Firmly, as a hospital Sister has learned to face everything. She was about to temporise with him—he looked ready to commit more of the same treatment that had put Mrs Bryan in hospital. But before she could say a word, she was thrust aside by an arm like an iron bar. She staggered, catching her shoulder against the other sandstone pillar, and could not help falling to her knees.

'Come on now!' the man snarled, grabbing Mrs Bryan. 'I've had enough of this nonsense. You're coming back where you belong. Home!'

'Let go of me!' Mrs Bryan cried. Struggling, but helpless.

'That's enough, I think.'

The new voice, incisive and commanding, brought the three of them looking at the newcomer.

Shelley could feel her mouth drop open, then found Colum Macadam's hand under her arm. He helped her to her feet, gently, but quite resolutely. 'Hurt?' He twitched his brows at her, and when she shook her head, turned to the smouldering Mr Bryan, still trying to drag his wife away.

'You stay out of this!' Bryan's mouth grew ugly, his eyes sweeping up and down Macadam's fine worsted suit, the smart necktie, the air of somebody about him. By comparison, Bryan looked as if he had raided a charity shop.

He shot a fist forward, intending to show this nosy newcomer who was in charge round here, then had the surprise of his life as a fist smashed into his chin, and he fell flat on his

47

back.

Shocked, he lay there for a moment, too amazed to realise what had happened. It was evident nobody treated Harry Bryan like that. He surged to his feet, about to charge forward, when the look he saw on Macadam's face stopped him. He shuffled uneasily, his face filled with rage, but made no further try at violence.

'If you're not out of sight in two minutes, I'll have you run in for assault,' Macadam threatened. He took a step forward, and Bryan shambled off.

'Sure you're not hurt?' Macadam asked Shelley again. He kept his hand on her arm as if he meant to give her a thorough examination there and then.

'Quite sure,' she said firmly, and detached the hand that seemed reluctant to let her go. 'I can stand quite well,' she assured him. Not for the world would she have him know what queer things the touch of that hand was doing to the cool, capable Sister Vyner. And how much she wanted that hand to keep holding her arm. If Mrs Bryan had not been there, she would have pretended to be much more shaken than she was, merely to have the luxury of that arm joined by the other one, and being held so close.

'Good God!' she thought, amazed at herself. 'I must be really shaken to go maundering like a teenager!'

It was Mrs Bryan who broke up the scene. She moved away a little, her womanly intuition telling her she had landed in a situation that did not really require her. In fact, required her to remove herself from the scene. She had caught only a glimpse of Shelley's face as Macadam held her arm, and felt a wretched intruder.

'Thank you for coming to my help, Mr Macadam,' she ventured.

He moved closer to her, took the hand she was holding out to him, and held it, quelling the instant jealousy Shelley felt by automatically taking her pulse, and examining her face as if he were conducting a bedside visit.

'I was coming to see you,' he explained. 'Had quite a job finding where you might be. I wanted to know how you were getting along.'

Turning to Shelley, he said, 'Remember, I was the one who did her pierced lung. I haven't seen her at my outpatient clinics. It was important to follow up her case.'

He looked at the shabby old house, tightened lips informing Shelley he knew all about its purpose.

'I've moved from my old place,' Mrs Bryan explained. 'I wanted to get clear away from my drunken husband. I just couldn't put up with any more of his drunken rages. Somebody must have told him I was here for a short time, and he turned up just as I was leaving.'

Macadam chuckled. 'I can see you are quite well, Mrs Bryan, but I would like to ask you a few more questions. Since you won't come to my clinics, I'll have to conduct this one outside the hospital. But not here, I think.' His gaze turned again to the big house, seeming to take in every detail of its worn sandstone facade, the blackened, drooping sycamore in the patch of garden, the sagging sign, already weathered beyond significance, announcing Elizabeth Fry House.

Macadam nodded, the sign holding his gaze for a moment. 'A nice touch, that. Elizabeth Fry, prison reformer. Especially for women.'

He took hold of them each by the arm—he seemed a great one for holding arms, Shelley thought, and realised she enjoyed it. She liked bodily contact with him, and wondered where the stiff-faced sister who had stood up so angrily to the equally stiff-faced surgeon had gone.

'We'll continue my questions at a more suitable rendezvous,' Macadam said firmly. 'My car, just across the road.'

He ushered them to a sleek Mercedes, neither too large nor too showy, but exactly right for the surgeon who wanted everything about him to be the best.

Some more suitable rendezvous turned out to be a smart restaurant a few minutes from a large car-park. A new place Shelley had thought of visiting but put off till she had more money to spare for less essentials.

Mrs Bryan baulked at the red-canopied entrance. 'Really,' she demurred. 'I ought to be going. I'm sure Sister would rather the two of you...'

'Consider this my temporary clinic,' Macadam said smoothly, manoeuvring them both inside, where the carpeted floor induced an immediate sense of luxury.

Shelley had a quick rise of temper. How dare he bring them here! A swift glance at the other late diners, rich businessmen from the dormitory suburb across the river, and their consorts, looking like covers from *Vogue*. And she—in the drab garb for her duty visits to the home for battered wives.

But the surroundings made more impact on Mrs Bryan than on Shelley. She almost shuffled forward to the table where the receptionist to the grill ushered them, a receptionist with a flawless complexion and the Titian hair she had always envied.

'Just a drink then, and I really will have to be on my way,' Mrs Bryan protested, as Macadam picked up the menu—the size of it alone would have scared a woman for whom British Home Stores cafe was a favourite place. 'The widow I'm living with plans to visit her mother, and she likes somebody in the flat.'

She would not be dissuaded. A few questions from Macadam, a quick glass of white wine, and she was on her feet, clutching her cheap handbag as if for protection, before scurrying across the olive-green carpet to freedom.

'You should not have brought us here,' Shelley rebuked him. She had got over her own reluctance to come to the place. After all, she was Sister Vyner, and any nurse who had done as many stints in Casualty as she had before her elevation to sister could cope with anything. But Mrs Bryan, bringing her here had been like taking a mouse through an alley full of cats.

'Where else? Burger King? MacDonald's?' His lips tightened. 'I wasn't always a consultant, with money for gracious living. I served my time to poverty and cheap lunches. Now, I want only the best out of life. I earn it, and I want it. And—' he grinned boyishly, 'seems we're dining out after all.'

'If you had asked my choice,' Shelley said coldly, 'I'd have opted for somewhere else.' She glanced round, as if noting for a second time how most of the couples at other tables seemed to be men quite a bit older than their companions. 'This looks to me like a convenient spot for businessmen to bring their secretaries.'

'Ah—so that's the reason for the look of disdain you've been wearing like a suit of armour since we arrived.' Macadam smiled. 'You're afraid people will think you and I are having an affair.' His smile widened, grew cynical. 'They little know our chaste young sister would never stoop to anything so sordid.'

'What do you mean!' Shelley had to stop herself throwing her glass of white wine in his face.

'All Barding knows you'd never do a thing like that. The sacred sister, current bearer of the sacred lamp.'

'I hate sneering people,' Shelley snapped. 'You embarrassed Mrs Bryan, and your remarks about me are the edge of enough. Or did you enjoy bringing me here to show me up against every other woman in the place?'

He looked blank. Then let his gaze roam the room. The chattering diners, the sense of ease and expensive enjoyment everywhere. Except in the cold-eyed sister facing him. 'From where I sit,' he said calmly, 'you are the best looking woman in the room. If it's your old mac draping the wooden reindeer for coats, forget it. There isn't a woman here who wouldn't willingly swap her finery for your complexion. Every second I sit here it is a temptation to lean over and run my finger down that lovely cheek, and round that beautiful jawline.'

He laughed, wore a look of unusual frustration. 'I'm a surgeon. My job is to cut people up then put them back the best way I can. I like it. It's what I was meant for. But there are times when I look at a beautiful woman and wish I were a painter instead, to get down something that unfortunately does not last, and so is so much the more precious while it is still there.'

His eyes gleamed with sardonic amusement as Shelley sat back, not shocked, but so surprised she could not find a word to say.

Somehow, she found a dish of starters on the table, something like a miniature Danish smorgasbord. Delicious, before she even began to sample the offerings.

'You have a wonderful way of telling me I'm going to be a withered old hag,' she said defensively. For the life of her she would not let him guess the sweep of wonder that swept through her as he had been speaking. For a moment she wished he had been snapping at her, the impatient, forward-looking surgeon who had no desires except business. He acted like a man who thought she was—she was . . . She refused to go on. It was too bewildering. Bogeymen did not change so quickly into Prince Charmings. Especially not this hard-jawed, stone-eyed man who was leaning back watching her with that familiar gleam of amusement in his eyes.

'This was the best place I could think of on the spur of the moment,' he said smoothly. 'The popular eating places Mrs Bryan would have preferred are all closed. Nor did I want to take you to a pub for pies and beer.' And his gaze swept her again, what was he looking for in her, she demanded of herself. Her heart was fluttering. Heavens, that was how it felt, though her nursing knowledge told her that hearts did not do that sort of thing. Not unless they were fibrillating. And she had no fear of that, not right now. She had never felt so alive, so excited at the thought of a new world that might be opening to her.

She realised with a sense of wonder that Macadam could project an aura of something else besides the dynamic surgeon who expected everything to make way for him. Like—like a magician, with the power to conjure up thrilling, wonderful things.

'And it did make sure Mrs Bryan did not stay too long,' he chuckled. 'I only wanted to ask her a few questions. And believe me, once she gets over her embarrassment at being with the nobs, she'll look back on her visit to this place as a high spot. And she'll feel really something at me chasing after her to find out how she felt after her operation.'

Seeing the questions forming in Shelley's eyes, he said, 'I am quite serious at following up my old patients. I happen to be writing a book on their recovery after tricky operations. Hers was a difficult case. I intend to cite her in my book.'

His smile was warm, embracing them both,

something for them to share. And she responded. She was afraid for herself. This Macadam did have a charm nobody would have guessed from his sharply efficient manner in the theatre. But she had had one devastating experience, where she had laid her young and vulnerable heart for a man to treasure, and he had almost wiped his feet on it. Never again she had sworn. And here she was, older—but God in heaven, apparently no wiser. That smile was hovering in front of her like a spell to entice her out of her sanctuary to experience once again the joys and pain of an affair.

It was the pain she was thinking of now, as she dropped her gaze. Colum seemed different. But could she take the risk. Cope with another episode that led to nothing. Unlike Jacqueline Susann she did not believe that 'Once was not enough.' Even once was too much.

Out of her reverie, she found the beef Stroganoff in front of her, and an amused Macadam still watching her. Was she going to figure in some zany book he wanted to write, she thought, growing hostile. She picked up her knife and fork. If he wanted just to amuse himself, break down the defences of the Women's Surgical sister, just to prove he could do it, she could kill him.

'I'm quite serious about the book.' He took the tension out of the moment by attacking his meal. Commented how good it was, and smiled cynically as Shelley retorted it was probably a boil-in-a-bag item since a lot of good restaurants now specialised in featured meals bought wholesale from manufacturers who made them by the carload.

She ate, wishing the situation did not confuse her so. She wanted him to be interested in her, as a woman, and not just as an efficient ward sister who could greatly facilitate his work. But who could place such trust in a man so obviously career-minded as Colum Macadam?

And what was he saying now? She came out of her thoughts again with a start, to find him regarding her with controlled patience.

'I said I was going to Japan as soon as I've finished my contract at Barding.'

'Japan!' All at once, the allure of the excellent beef Stroganoff disappeared. She stared, while a wealth of disappointment broke in her. 'Japan!' she murmured again. 'Whatever for? I've never figured you for a cherry-blossom lover.'

'I've another book in mind,' he told her. 'It's over forty years now since Hiroshima and Nagasaki. Since then, children have been born whose parents were affected by the bombs. I want to find out what effect it all had on the bones of their children. To see if they offer any special problems for surgeons. Enough time has elapsed to get a four-square look at the situation.'

He spoke so matter-of-factly Shelley was appalled. It sounded so cold-blooded, ferreting about in the dismal aftermath of a tragedy.

He leaned forward, voice low, serious. 'Their problems will eventually affect us all. The beginnings of it are apparent even now. How are people in general going to be injured by the increased radiation all over the world? All these nuclear plants springing up in every country. No matter how the different authorities pooh-pooh the dangers, every plant leaks in one way or another. I want to find out if people are facing more risks than they realise. And Japan is a good place to start.' I'm wondering if it is to be "Sayonara, sweet sister."'

'Sayonara?' Shelley was startled.

'Japanese for "Goodbye." It's been through my mind that it would be a good idea to have an efficient assistant with me, especially one with experience like yours. So it might not be a case of "Sayonara," Sister Shelley. Perhaps you could come with me.'

'Come with you? Leave Barding?'

'Why not?' The sea grey eyes bored into her. 'You've got to leave some time.'

CHAPTER FOUR

Of course it was utterly ridiculous. What on earth would she do in Japan? If Macadam really were serious, about all she could do was hold his hand, and take a few notes while he made his clinical surveys of people.

But then, he couldn't be serious. He was having a joke at her expense. Her mouth crinkled into a reluctant smile. It was hard to imagine the stern-faced Macadam teasing.

Japan! Cherry-blossom. The magnificent Fujiyama, sacred to every Japanese. The beautiful gardens, where they tried to create a haven where the physical could blend with the spiritual.

'Is that all right, Sister?'

The anxious voice broke through her reverie, and brought her back to the present. Cherry-blossom seemed a world away from the ward, where she had been supervising Nurse Little prepare a bed for its new occupant, a young girl. Shelley recalled the name with an effort, not yet fully released from the silly vapourings she had been entertaining. Japan, indeed!

'Perfect.' Shelley smiled her approval. Every article of bedding meticulously in place, folded along the length of the bed, waiting for the new patient to be slid deftly on to the waiting sheet.

Nurse Little beamed. The ward sister was so far above her in Barding's hierarchy any crumb of praise was treasured.

'I'd hate to have my appendix out,' Nurse Little confessed. She glanced round at the other occupants of the ward, reading, chatting across the beds, happy to have had the morning round over, and the consultants with their train of white coats and bothersome questions gone to moider somebody else. They had all had, or were going to have, much more complicated operations than a mere appendix, but to Nurse Little, darkly attractive, a nineteen-year-old with an appendix was too close to her in age not to assume an added importance. Only old women had hysterectomies and things, Nurse Little thought, with youth's carefree attitude that anybody over twenty-five was already on the slow creep to the grave.

'You going to the garden party, Sister?' she asked, eyes bright with wanting to know. There had been a rumour, instantly squashed, because Sister Immaculate would never do such a thing, that somebody had seen her going into the high-nosh feeding-place in town with Colum Macadam.

If she could glean a fragment of news, Little thought, eyes brighter still, it would make her the most listened-to in her set.

'I expect so,' Shelley murmured absently,

60

watching the door. She could expect the arrival of Carol Eddy any moment. She had been phoned from theatre, and once the girl had been installed, Shelley could get back to her office and the inevitable paper work. She would not have been doing this routine work, but her sturdy back-up, Karen Barnwell, had phoned in sick.

'Going with anybody?' Nurse Little asked innocently, big sapphire eyes trying not to look hopeful.

Deep inside her, Shelley loosed a chuckle. She was not taken in by that dewy-eyed innocence. She had had it once herself, and had been pushed by her set to find out what she could about Sister Tute's alleged romance with an anaesthetist who had been borrowed for a week or two from their rival, St Mark's.

'I am, actually,' Shelley went on, her attention still occupied with people passing up and down the passage outside. Apparently unaware of Nurse's Little's sharp interest, she let a few more moments elapse before she could say, 'I'm giving Sister Marron a lift. She doesn't have a car, and where she lives, buses are very awkward.'

Chuckling to herself, she made for her office. She would pop out again when the comatose young Carol was brought in, although she really did not have to be present. But it gave her younger nurses confidence if she was on hand.

She could imagine the disgusted manner with which Nurse Little's news about Sister's companion to the garden party would be received. Nothing fell flatter than a brick except a piece of exploded gossip.

An hour later, Shelley was startled by the cool voice whose echo had been running through her head most of the morning. Through her mind like a herd of startled gazelles stampeded the speculations that this routine visit of Macadam would start round the ward. And she damned the sudden uprush of colour from her trimly collared neck. God, like a pallid student trembling her first entry through the doors of PTS.

'I'd just like a glance at Carol Eddy,' Macadam said. He stood there, filling the doorway, one hand on the jamb, as if to suggest that this office, and whatever was in it, was his.

Past his shoulder, Shelley could see down the ward, where Nurse Little was standing with a just-recovered bedpan from Mrs Carey, the cervical-cancer patient. Holding the covered thing like a triumphant trophy, while her bright eyes and twitching nose contrived to make the attractive girl into something like a white-capped ferret.

Shelley laid down her pen. She was warmed by the way Macadam always referred to his patients by name. He was very particular about the patients as people, with identities as well as temporary afflictions. Not all surgeons bothered.

They stood together, by Carol's bed, just observing. It was another of Macadam's habits. He always visited his patients before they had recovered from the anaesthetic. He liked to get the feel of them, he had informed Shelley, as if he thought she might be critical.

'I think she'll do,' Macadam ventured. 'She'll soon be up and around, planning her next trip to her local disco.'

They walked back to Shelley's office, and all the time she was acutely aware of gazes following them. She was inwardly furious. After their initial brush, she had achieved what she thought was a good working relationship with the surgeon, and now there was this speculation spreading to upset those same easy relations. Probably, she thought bitterly, it would be relayed to the doctors' lounge, where some brash young medic would be fool enough to chaff Macadam about his success with Sister Immaculate.

And now here was this idiot actually inviting her to go to the garden party with him!

'I've never been to one before,' Macadam confessed, sitting on the corner of her desk with the ease of one who had sat there a hundred times. No other doctor had ever taken such a liberty, she thought, incensed, then had to admit that with no risk of gossip

63

she would have very much liked him sitting there, with that comfortable ease between them. How could she ever have thought him stone-faced! But that human ferret, Nurse Little, would be watching. And there she was, for heaven's sake, with those so-innocent eyes flicking unheard messages to Nurse Rhodes.

And all at once here was the ferret herself. 'Is it all right for Mrs Mason to go to the day-room, Sister?' she asked.

'Of course, Nurse. She'll be glad if you walk with her, her first time out of bed. Just warn her not to be on her feet too long.'

'Yes, Sister, thank you, Sister.' Nurse Little was off, but not before her lingering glance took in every aspect of Colum Macadam, and afforded him a discreet little flutter of her lashes that were too long for any male's peace of mind.

'There should be a law against young temptresses like that,' Macadam chuckled.

'There are several,' Shelley said stiffly. 'Not that too many people observe them these days.'

She remembered only too well the numerous rape cases brought in to Casualty when she was on duty there.

There were a few things to discuss with Macadam, but they were soon discussed enough for Shelley to wonder why Macadam was still hanging around. She had never known him so willing to linger. Always before, it had been like an itinerary of the Queen, everything programmed to the exact minute. It couldn't be, could it, that he was working up to something? She'd had the experience of quite a few young doctors dithering about her office, trying to whip themselves up to asking her out. And not a few brash medics who had rushed it head on, mincing no words. But surely a consultant with the drive and decisiveness of Colum Macadam could not be afflicted with nerves.

'Fancy a trip to the seaside?' he asked abruptly, swinging round from the wall where a lavish display of notices and work routines were pinned. The slightest twitch of his lips made her sure he had absorbed every detail of the working-arrangements of the ward for the next month.

'Friday evening?' Again the smile, not diffident, not teasing, just very provocative, daring her. As if to say he was offering something he did not offer just at random, and if she turned him down, in keeping with her cool refusal of other such invitations, he could easily find a more accommodating companion. And Lord knows, that not cocky but well justified assumption of his desirability was well merited. If a line formed of those who would jump at such a chance to be squired by Macadam it would stretch beyond the hospital gates.

His smile did taunt her. 'You have three days to find a good excuse,' he rallied her.

'Why should I need an excuse?' She would have liked to take the wind out of his sails by refusing there and then. Plain, blank 'No!' But an imp of indulgence urged her to delay outright refusal. She wanted to go. Nor was she at all particular where they went. Just so long as this irritating, maddening man was with her, they could tour a bunch of empty warehouses in dockland, and it would be just as exhilarating as a candlelit dinner.

She almost giggled, but her role as Sister Immaculate easily prevented that. And she frowned mentally as she thought that she had never wished to be known by such a name, but now that she had it, she would rather like to keep it. After all, it did lift her out somewhat from the rather grey band of the other sisters.

She hardly knew how she came to utter the words. But they were out before she had time to wonder. 'I suppose there is a business side to this invitation?'

The smile of gratification that showed he had read her correctly needled her. This man was getting to know her too well.

'There is, and there isn't,' he agreed. 'I want a few hours away from the hospital, somewhere I can hear the sea washing up on the sand, listen to the scraping sound it makes going out again, and listen to seagulls

66

where they ought to be, instead of swarming over the towns. Does that sound foolish?'

'Not at all.' Shelley fingered the file nearest her, knowing she ought to cut this short, that already he had stayed too long with her, stirring up further gossip for Nurse Little to spread, but she felt reluctant to let him go. He need be in no hurry because his round was over, and he had no clinics till the afternoon. And she felt a sudden surge of defiance against the rigid rules she had mapped out for herself ever since becoming a sister.

'And there is a professional aspect. One of my former patients lives near St Anne's. Nice place. We got acquainted after I removed a growth, and have kept in close touch ever since. I visit him about every three months. We talk, stroll on the beach—it's never crowded. Not quite near enough the popular resorts. Enjoy the sea air. This time, I'm sure he would not feel neglected if I chose to do the strolling bit with you instead.'

'Very well.' Shelley reached abruptly for the file. This had gone on too long already. And could hardly keep her voice at its usual cool evenness as they were interrupted again.

Sandra Rhodes this time, Nurse Little's first-year companion. Fat and youthfully eager, belt straining against her middle. She was forever cheerful, and there was no guile in her light blue eyes as she asked Shelley, 'Is there anything special you wanted me to do,

Sister?'

'Not right now, thank you, Nurse.' Shelley got up swiftly. That scheming young Little! The prompting of Nurse Rhodes' bumbling inquiry had undoubtedly come from her. Probably giggling out of sight in the sluice, waiting eagerly for a report on what was going on in the office.

'I'll be with you in a minute,' Shelley stressed, going towards the door. 'Mr Macadam is leaving.'

A little devil of mischief laced his voice as he followed her out. ''Bye for now, Sister. See you Friday.'

He went past Nurse Rhodes, dropping the fleetest of smiles on her as he moved past.

She would have spoken, but a look at Shelley's stiffening face deterred her. She smiled sheepishly, and scurried down the ward.

Shelley wished for once she was not a sister, but a carefree nurse like her staff. So she could stand with them, bright-eyed and bursting with enough delight she wanted to share it with them. But she was past that stage. Now she had an image to maintain. It was invaluable to her as a sister, making nurses eager to work with her, and still more eager to do well there. She had to appear as calm and efficiently minded as always. For a moment she wondered what the patients and nurses would think if she suddenly threw her neatly frilled cap in the air. For that was how she felt.

★   ★   ★

Macadam was reluctant to allow Shelley time to go back to her flat to change from her uniform. But he acknowledged that perhaps it would be better for them to meet outside the hospital.

'There's enough gossip about us already,' she warned. 'Opening your mouth to let Nurse Rhodes know what we were doing. Don't you know it is absolutely out of character for us to take off like a couple of carefree youngsters in the first throes?'

'Is that what we are?' he inquired, again that devil of mischief in his eyes. 'And whatever are throes?'

'That's how it would look if we drove off from Barding together,' she assured him. 'Don't you realise what a reputation you have? A workaholic, stacking up successful cases like shelves in a supermarket. Hardly time to say "Good morning".'

'Is that how I looked?' Genuine interest replaced the taunt in his eyes. 'Well, while we're doing "This Is Your Life," perhaps you ought to accept the fact you're the biggest wonder. Sister Immaculate. No time for doctors.'

He measured her, surprising her by the

69

kindness of his gaze. 'Did it hurt very much?'

'Hurt—what?' She looked away, then sank back against the cool leather. 'Yes,' she admitted. She knew what he was referring to. It had sliced a piece from her heart she was sure would never be replaced. Even now, so long after, she could not hear the name Chris without remembering that racking time at Wellingborough coming back to her. The Mercedes purred smoothly along the secondary road, giving them time to enjoy the untroubled greenery and the trees that stood there at irregular intervals, declaring there was still unspoiled countryside away from the hustling motorways.

'What took your mind away from strictly business?' Shelley asked abruptly, breaking a silence that had settled on them. Not that she was disturbed by that silence. They were comfortable with each other, no need of talk to fill every minute. She just wanted to probe the mystery of this man who had first antagonised her, then reached out with invisible links so that now she was vastly interested in him. Both as a surgeon and—there was no sense trying to hide it from herself—sexually. It had been a long time, and she admitted to herself that whatever was promised in that long figure beside her, his hands so effortlessly but skilfully on the wheel, made her thoughts spiral into regions they had been a stranger to for too long.

She remembered once, when she was about ten, when she had captured a greenfinch that had wandered into the house. She could feel its heart beating in its breast like a tiny thunder, vibrating against her fingers. Now her own heart felt like that long-gone bird's, only there was an exciting tilt to the way hers was beating. If she had been alone she could have laughed for sheer joy.

'You!'

His answer was so completely unexpected, so briefly certain, Shelley's breath caught. And she was silent, stunned by his sincerity. Glad to remain so until they reached the house where his old patient lived.

Jonathan Ivers was a tall, spare man, with a studied way of speaking, as if being a bachelor, living alone, he wanted each word to mean something.

Shelley had encountered it before, with widows, who had been forced to adjust to having nobody there to listen to them. It was as if they valued the unaccustomed contact so much that everything they had to say had to be of value.

He lived in a new development in the seaside town, a goodish way from the seafront. Just far enough for a nice walk each morning, he revealed, faded blue eyes twinkling. A few things to buy then a sojourn in the town's new library, where comfortable

71

tables and chairs made reading something to be enjoyed.

Shelley did not need this measured ambience explained. She had known of widows having to make their adjustments, who settled into such day-devouring routines that kept loneliness at bay.

He was disgustingly well, Ivers assured them, submitting cheerfully to Macadam's swift examination, once half laughingly telling Shelley he would have been dead these last three years but for the doctor cutting away the malignancy that threatened him.

'Every day from then I've owed to Doctor Mac,' he said with simple gratitude. 'I'll never forget. I'll be in your book, won't I, Doctor?'

He smiled them away, and for the first time Shelley realised just what the book meant to Macadam.

He chaffed her. 'You didn't really believe I was going to do it, did you?'

'Well,' she murmured defensively, 'I've met a lot of doctors who are always talking about the books they mean to write when they get a chance to really get at it. The book that's going to be the definitive work on everything from mumps to liver-rebuilding. Somehow, they never quite crystallise.'

'And you thought I was one of those.' Macadam's voice was light enough, but she did not have to look at him to know his brows were tight-pinched. She was startled to realise how well she was beginning to know this man. If she had had any artistic talent she could have limned his face from memory.

He did not allow her time to say more, but turned in his seat as he cut off the engine and grasped the hand that was lying loosely across her lap. 'I am a very serious fellow. I never say anything I don't mean.'

A silence that lasted for a few seconds, but throbbed with meaning. 'Or do anything without a good reason.'

Did his fingers tighten on hers? She could not really say. All she knew was that for a few brief seconds his eyes held hers and said things that she only half understood, but left her pulse stirring to a quicker, more exhilarating rhythm.

'Time for our paddle,' he laughed. Measuring her again, half mocking, half daring. 'Or are you still Sister Immaculate, who wouldn't dream of walking barefoot in the sea?'

She could not help the colour that washed to her forehead. She felt like a vapid student, smarting from a rebuke from Sister Tute. She could not believe how easily this man stripped away any pretensions she had to being in complete control of herself. He only had to look at her, with that taunting, provoking smile . . .

'That stupid nickname!' she said cuttingly

restoring some equanimity to herself. 'Just because...!' She faced him squarely. 'A sister has to guard her reputation, especially a young one. Gossip can spread like wildfire.'

'Didn't I take care to meet you outside office hours?' he mocked. 'Did I not take scrupulous care over your lily-white reputation? But there's nobody from Barding within fifty miles! Let's go paddle.'

The first wish-wash of salt water over her feet made Shelley gasp, then her spirits lifted magically as Macadam slipped his arm through hers, and led her a few feet further into the rapidly ebbing tide.

Warm now, once she got used to it, the water seemed to wash away every last little niggle. As for Macadam—Colum! She could not go on thinking of him as Macadam, the career-thrusting surgeon, not when he was laughing with such high spirits as vagrant waves slapped impishly at them.

'Enough!' He guided her away from the water, laughing down at her sparking eyes. 'Paddling is like ice-cream. Just enough is marvellous. Too much, a drag.'

She sat on the low stone wall that bordered the beach, brushing futilely at the sand that still clung to her feet.

'This is the worst of reverting to childhood games,' she said, half cross. 'I hate sand between my toes!'

'If Madame will just wait a few moments,'

Colum assured her gravely, 'all will be well.'

She watched him walk back to the ebbing water, carrying a bowl he had thoughtfully carried in the boot.

And when he came back, to leave the filled bowl of water beside her, he retrieved a brightly coloured towel from where he had got the bowl.

'Oh, so you came prepared?' Shelley chaffed.

'Why not? I like sea water on my feet. We should all keep one of the magical things of childhood to remind us. This is my particular rave.'

He was kneeling, and lifted one of her legs by the ankle, resting her foot in the water. Then the other, and with the same care he gave to his work in the theatre, proceeded to wash the sand from her feet.

Shelley sat very still. Looking down at his bent head, she had to clasp her hands tightly in her lap, to stop herself fondling the thick black hair that clung to his head like a crusader's helmet. It was an urge that pulsed through her like a warning signal, and did nothing to stop the trembling that threatened to display itself to him, as her stomach filled with fluttering butterflies.

His fingers were solicitously tender, as if he handled something too precious to mar. Nor could she deny the delicious ripple of anticipation that did nothing to restore her to sober calm. Sister Immaculate, indeed! If he could only guess what she was thinking!

Looking up unexpectedly, he must have caught something in her face, for his smile grew from simple pleasure as he held one of her feet to a mockery that threatened her contrived calm.

'Scared?' he asked, a devil of merriment in his eyes.

'Should I be?' she challenged, feeling things were proceeding undesirably fast, for this was a public beach. Several families were scattered around, with children, a few young couples, and her plunging thoughts were not for family viewing.

'I feel like the Pope,' Colum said, easing the moment.

'I feel more like King Cophetua and the beggar maid,' Shelley laughed. She looked away, out to sea where a couple of rust-coloured sails showed two shrimping-boats making their way home.

How marvellous the simplest things were when the right person was doing them. She wished for this moment to go on for ever, but she realised sadly that the magic was in the moments; prolonged, boredom would set in.

There was no lingering in the way Macadam restored his own feet to the state needed to slip on socks and shoes. He tossed away the sandy water, restored bowl and towel to the boot, and faced her.

76

'I was thinking,' he said softly, 'there's time for us to pay a fleeting visit to my house on the way back. Or would you rather...?'

'Why not?' She was frankly keen to see where he lived, and how. She had assumed he was not married, but had never really speculated about any other female interest. Now, she felt a stirring of pleasure, at seeing some of the secrets of Colum Macadam revealed.

'I bought it just before I moved to Barding,' he told her, driving back to the main road. Carefully, for day trippers and residents seemed to assume that in this seaside place the road was theirs as much as the pavements. Anyway why irritate them with bad tempered horn-blowing, Shelley thought? They got out of the way good naturedly, as the Mercedes nudged along, some of the children waving cheerfully. Even some lingering looks from women holding on to children's hands, as if to envy such a good looking and happily matched couple.

They sat in silence in the front of the bungalow where Macadam finally brought the Mercedes to rest. It was the first in a line of detached houses on the fringe of Barding. Trees lined one side of the road, pleasurably away from the front gardens. There was a sense of space about the neighbourhood, a graceful simplicity in the gardens and the red-brick houses that backed them.

Particularly the bungalow that Macadam had bought. Perhaps if the curtains were—Shelley caught herself up abruptly. What had it to do with her? As it was, the bungalow was perfectly satisfactory, especially since it belonged to a bachelor. She could not help wondering, with a touch of jealousy, if he had a housekeeper, or a woman to come in and clean.

'I could just about manage the mortgage, it's convenient for work, and I like it. Neighbours, but not close enough to be bothered with requests for a cup of sugar,' Macadam said almost smugly.

Shelley hid a smile. When the neighbours got to know a little more about the desirable bachelor so close to them, they would certainly contrive some cunning excuses to intrude on his privacy.

'Coffee?' he suggested. 'Only Nescafe, but nicely drinkable. Or don't you believe Gareth Hunt?'

It should have been a delightful interlude, but somehow, it was strangled by a tension that suddenly came on them from nowhere.

Shelley could understand why she gripped the handle of her cup too intensely. Without any stupid jokes about etchings, somehow, the ease between them had been destroyed.

She was overwhelmingly conscious that what she really wanted, instead of sitting here sipping coffee which she did not really want, was for him to carry her upstairs in the macho piratical style so beloved of romantic bodice-busters and throw her upon his bed.

But—and she could barely repress the giggle that all at once rose unbidden to her throat—he did not even have an upstairs! He had a bungalow. Lord, what a passion-smasher!

She got up quickly, carelessly upsetting her bag, tipping some of the contents on to the carpet.

Stooping hurriedly, she found her head cracking against Macadam's, as he too tried to retrieve her belongings. The entertaining thoughts Shelley had been diverted with disappeared into a sense of *opéra bouffe*. All they needed she thought, suppressing another urge to laugh, was a pair in a horse-costume to come galloping in, pursued by a red-nosed comedian.

'I'm sorry.' Macadam threw up his hands. He frowned, then had to laugh. 'I guess it wasn't such a good idea after all,' he echoed her thoughts. 'I ought not to have stopped.'

He helped her to her feet, and without pausing, went out to the car. She followed, anticlimax a dead weight in her. Stifling a sense of rejection. When she had agreed to come here, she had to be honest and admit it was not coffee she wanted. But he had drawn back. At the last minute decided not to take whatever he had in mind any further.

Was it Japan, she wondered? Was he thinking of Japan, needing for his own reasons to go alone, guessing she would have been more than willing to go with him, and to blazes with Barding's gossips? That all too soon, it would indeed be a case of Sayonara, sweet sister, and she would be left like Madame Butterfly, without even the satisfaction of having had a love affair.

CHAPTER FIVE

The Mercedes slipped smoothly away from Macadam's bungalow, seeming to mock them with its silken progress. Each had their own thoughts, and Shelley mused that if Macadam's were as tangled as hers, he might very well be provoked by the effortless way the car sped along.

She was in such a fret with herself she longed to be alone, somewhere she could kick cushions around. What she had built herself up to, and the ridiculous anticlimax. Bumping heads when they should have been locked in passionate embrace.

Sister Immaculate, indeed! If he only knew what storms had raged behind her serene demeanour. How she longed to run with him in a madcap burst in the moonlight, then sink into his embrace, the silvery light framing them in benevolent sympathy. She wished she could write. From what was tumbling through her mind she could turn out a sizzler!

She was aware all at once of a muffled oath from Macadam. A tension that whipped her senses to frightening clarity. They had been approaching a steep hill, the secondary road they were travelling on not yet burrowing into the busyness of the city. Halfway down the hill was a huge lorry piled with sand. Horn tooting desperately, it was plain the driver was in trouble. Doing his best to haul his great load to a halt by muscle power alone.

Yards ahead of the runaway lorry a small car was trying to keep ahead of the danger. And a few yards in front of their Mercedes a new Rover was hooting madly, as if by sound alone the threatened smash could be averted.

One side of the road was a tilted grass slope. The other, a stretch of grass and weeds that edged on to a cow pasture.

Macadam swung on to the grass, brakes pulling hard. He stopped within inches of a post-and-wire fence, and was out of the car in a flash.

Sound filled the air like a sudden gale. Shelley saw the lorry at the foot of the hill make a desperate swerve to avoid the car in front. The manoeuvre was too sudden to succeed. It missed the small Fiat still trying to avoid being run down, grazed the Rover, and sent it by sheer momentum raking on to

81

the grass, where it scraped a wing against the stationary Mercedes.

Overturned, the lorry shed sand everywhere. Glass cracked and split as the cab of the vehicle dragged a slow path down the slope where it had finished its runaway.

By this time, Shelley joined Macadam where he had succeeded in reaching the lorry-driver, dragged at his belt, and was tugging him free.

'I've got him!' Macadam said tersely. 'Look at the others!'

'They're all right!' She was just as abrupt. She had glimpsed both drivers rigid with shock over their wheels, but both apparently unhurt. Time enough for them later.

Even as she was helping Macadam extricate the lorry-driver, the man from the Rover was stumbling towards them, white-faced, but willing to do what he could. He stopped for a word with the driver of the Fiat, a woman, then carried on to the lorry.

The sudden slide of the heavy vehicle off the road had shifted its load of sand. Somehow, sand had burst into the cab, half smothering the driver, stifling his cries.

And now Macadam was having to keep pushing it away as it interfered with his rescue. The sheer weight of the stuff kept it sifting through the big slit in the back of the cab. Blowing back her hair which persisted in falling across her eyes, Shelley had her own troubles with the stuff. It was everywhere.

'Can you hold the door back?' she gasped to the Rover driver. By now, Macadam had squirmed his way into the cab, somehow managing to get behind the driver, further able to help Shelley in getting the man to safety.

It was easier once the other man could help. Looking like a rising young executive in his well cut grey suit, he was pale-faced from shock, but functioning capably, replacing Shelley so that his superior strength finally managed to pull the driver from the cab.

He was unconscious, a nasty gash looking worse than it probably was seeping blood to join the mess on his face.

'I'll call an ambulance,' the Rover-driver suggested, standing back from where Macadam was giving the lorry-driver an examination. 'I've got one of those phones in my car. If it's still working.'

Not waiting for an answer, he hurried away, made two ineffective tugs at the door before he got it open. Still shaky from what might have happened, he reached for the phone. The convenience of success, he told himself, and luckily, so very convenient in this case.

Leaving Macadam to look after his patient, Shelley joined the woman in the small Fiat. She was just sitting in her seat, white and drawn, obviously glad of another woman to

83

help her readjust.

'No, I'm not hurt,' she professed shakily. 'Just stiff with fright. I was struck rigid when I realised that lorry was out of control. I thought I was going to be a paragraph in tomorrow's papers. Tearing down the hill after me—I suppose the brakes had gone. And you and the other car! I just didn't know what to—to do!'

'It's over now,' Shelley told her gently, holding the woman's arm to stop her shivering. It was all Shelley could do to stop herself from a few shudders. If she had been in this tiny Fiat, she would have been even more shocked.

She took the woman's matches from her trembling hands, and struck a match for her cigarette. Government health warnings were all very well, but there were cases when a cigarette worked better than a sedative drug.

By the time the woman had caught hold of herself, and managed to impart some of her private life to Shelley—a shock like this always seemed to have a loosening effect, Shelley knew—the ambulance had arrived. Heartening white, with its orange-red streaks on the side.

She watched with professional interest as the lorry driver was loaded into the ambulance—under the equally alert eyes of the police car's occupants who had just arrived.

They then surveyed the scene of the accident with unhappy eyes. Once they had garnered an account of the accident from Macadam—so obviously able to give an orderly account—there would be a lot to do.

All that sand over the road. Traffic inevitably building up. Impatient drivers getting red-faced like most motorists when their right of way is challenged.

At last, Macadam was free. He joined Shelley, spread his hands in defeat. 'Well, there'll be no getting past that lot for half an hour or so. And if we don't get a move on, there'll be 'No Go' signs all over the place.'

He looked at her, smiled like an army scout perceiving the way out of an ambush. 'Only one sensible thing to do. Nip back to my place while we've still got the chance. All right with you?'

Shelley hesitated. She really ought to get home. She hadn't bargained for such a simple trip becoming so complicated.

'Take a look at yourself.' Macadam pointed to the wing mirror. 'A quick glimpse,' he chaffed.

Reaching a hand automatically to her hair, Shelley stopped halfway. Heavens! She looked a sight! Hair like demented seaweed. Muddy smears all over her face.

'You can clean up back home,' Macadam comforted her. He flicked a finger at the ivory-coloured linen suit she had worn with such satisfaction. So very fetching for a run to the sea—but for digging a man out of a load of sand ...!

'I'll lend you some jeans, and a pullover,' Macadam laughed. 'Roll up the legs and sleeves, and you'll look like one of those gay young things in the TV adverts.'

His chuckle was deep, inviting confidences. 'I can hardly say you live up to your nickname of Sister Immaculate now,' he said as he opened the passenger door for her.

His fingers lingered as he helped her inside, as if he were reluctant to let go of her.

It was only by a great effort she repressed the shudder that threatened to run through her. Sister Immaculate indeed! If only he knew of the storm that raged behind her serene demeanour. Honed and polished by years of coping with bad-tempered consultants and vinegary older nurses jealous of her looks, she needed all that composure now to prevent Macadam from seeing how she felt.

It was a relief to fuss with the sand that hissed from her clothes as she relaxed against the Mercedes' leather seat, and wriggled her neck against the collar of her blouse. It released the tension from her, allowed her a smile that rippled into open laughter as Macadam too, squirmed in his clothes.

For a moment, as she stood on the threshold of his house, she paused, relishing

86

the feel of the place closing round her. She had never felt so welcome anywhere. It was as if the house itself was glad to see her. As if she had a place here. There was a nick in the otherwise spotless white paint on the door to the lounge that she automatically decided needed a touch-up, and she could not help the disappointment when she told herself it was nothing to do with her. It was not her house. And very likely never would be. Macadam was too young to get tied up in marriage. Not with his ambitions. After all, at the moment, the thing mostly on his mind was his proposed trip to Japan.

A whole new world was waiting for him there. Those delicate Japanese women—some of them so perfect, so terribly attractive in their petite charm to a big man like Macadam. He could have supplanted John Wayne in the Geisha and the Sailor, or whatever was the title of that film she had seen once so long ago, and been perfect for the role.

Macadam followed her into the lounge, already throwing off his jacket on to the nearest chair.

'I feel filthy,' he complained, gingerly fingering his neck. He nodded to the small table in the corner. 'There's a bottle of Montrachet a too friendly liquor-store man off-loaded on to me. Maybe it should have been stored in the fridge, but I'm sure the people who made the stuff drink it any time any place without bothering with all that. It will save messing about with tea or coffee.'

He brought the drinks to where Shelley was still standing in the middle of the room. She felt too uncomfortable to sit. What she wanted was a bath, or a shower, anything, to feel herself clean and comfortable again. But it was not her place—though if he did not suggest something in the next sixty seconds...

'To your bright eyes, Sister,' Macadam touched his glass lightly to hers, and something in his gaze changed. The merest flicker, but it was like a sudden push to her heart, as if it had been bumping along steadily in a get-the-day-over-with pattern, and all at once had been electrified into a crazy gallop.

'You know, you are positively beautiful,' he said softly, each word a subtle caress. She could almost feel his hands on her body, lingering like a lover's kisses, and she was not at all surprised when he took her barely sipped glass and put it alongside his on the table, and kissed her lightly, but so convincingly.

It was as if all at once every inhibition she had ever had had been suddenly swept together, and tossed away like old books used to say about tossing bonnets over the nearest windmill.

He brushed lightly at a small area of dust that nestled teasingly at the lovely curve where her neck settled into her shoulder. And his fingers sought the buttons that closed her blouse over a bra so ridiculously flimsy it was only there for a sexy tease, as she had very well known when she bought it.

Her breath was coming in little gasps, as if puzzling what she was going to do next. But there was no hesitancy about the way her own fingers loosed his tie, and freed it from the collar of his shirt.

Fine sand fell in tiny grains about her, as she opened his shirt, and for one head-spinning moment rested her cheek against the solid muscle of his chest. She could have named the muscles there in strictly anatomical fashion, but at that moment she was not a nurse, but a woman unable to stop herself easing the shirt free of his shoulders.

And it was as inevitable as the sun rising each day when they were freed of their clothes, his hands hesitating over the last gossamer wisp of silk that freed her completely, as if it were the final act in a series, each one the whisper of love.

They were silent as they stood close to each other, breathing in each other's essence, loving each other. He picked her up, one hand under her thighs, not hurrying, enjoying to the full each careful movement

89

against the silken skin.

She was vibrantly aware of being in his arms, held close, a precious possession, wanting to hold that moment for ever, yet being impelled by an irresistible urge to open yet another door.

At his bedroom, she turned her face to him, kissed that mouth that had beckoned to her from the first. 'A shower,' she whispered, and as he followed her request, each step building a symphony of desire, she felt her love swell through her.

The water cascaded over them, tickling them, stirring them to laughter that gasped to a silence broken only by the hiss of water, and the little gasps as they kissed and separated.

They soaped each other, loving every caress, swilled and dried—and hardly waiting to finish the job were on the bed, straining to each other as they discovered new sources of enchantment.

*   *   *

Macadam made the coffee, a simple job of pouring boiling water on a good helping of Nescafe. By that time, Shelley had buttered thick slices of French bread, and whipped up an omelette with a filling of chives and thinly sliced tomatoes, and enough cheese to make the fluffily golden omelette look like a small whale.

She halved it expertly, slid them both on to plates, and joined Macadam at the formica-topped table he confessed to using for his lone meals, too daunted to eat alone in the living dining-room-module so expertly termed by estate agents' garble.

'I like to see a girl with a healthy appetite,' Macadam observed, as she reached for the last slice of bread.

'It would be hard to find a nurse with anything else!' Shelley retorted. 'Digging that poor man out made me ravenous.' She looked up. 'I wonder how he is.'

'We'll give him a ring later,' Macadam said lazily, pushing his chair back and stretching. Content, he gazed at her. 'Pity I don't smoke. A meal like that calls for a cigar.'

'Meal!' Shelley stared. 'A scratch thing like that!'

'How many eggs did you use? You served up a real plate-filler.' And in the same conversational tone, 'You'll be staying the night, I suppose?'

Shelley's brows rose. 'I hadn't planned on it.' An enticing vision of the bed already shared rose in her, and she looked away. She had not planned what happened before. It had just crept up on her, on them both, an involuntary interlude wholly enjoyable. At the time, irresistible. But to continue...

'Why not?' she said simply. 'I dare say the floor will be comfortable enough for you, if you use the cushions from the settee.'

'I had other ideas about a cushion,' he took her up lightly. He stood up. 'I'll give the hospital a ring. See what's happening.'

But he remained looking at her, saying nothing, but seeking a commitment if she wanted, not too eager, but certainly offering something more than a snatched affair of a couple of weeks in a crowded calendar.

When he rejoined her, he said, 'Comfortable.' They exchanged half-smiles, then burst out laughing. 'I'll bet the chap feels completely shattered, rather than comfortable. Now I know what it feels like from the patient's end.'

As she half sat up, she had to admit the settee he had bought for this room was sinfully luxurious. He went on, 'When is your next date at the battered wives' hideout? I'm thinking if that damned hooligan who was ready to do you a damage is lurking around again, maybe I'd better come with you.'

'Doctor,' Shelley gasped, 'that is positively the most romantic proposal I have ever had. What do you suggest I wear?'

'Boxing gloves, unless you've got a black belt hidden away.' He grew more serious. 'I've been doing some forward thinking. I hardly think I'll be ready to say "Sayonara" when the time comes. How about you?'

Shelley took another sip of the wine he had poured. Nothing to sing songs about, but

92

pleasant enough. 'A lot of things can happen before your proposed trip,' she said slowly. 'Let's just say I'd love to see Japan at cherry-blossom time.' She got up quickly. 'I think I'd better go home. It has been very nice,' she went on, deliberately understating what had been a haunting enchanting episode, but it all seemed to be happening too quickly. For a time, she and Macadam had shared something exquisite. She was wise enough not to want to repeat it too quickly. After all, he would not be the first man to propose something like this, then get second thoughts before really committing himself.

He did not argue. He joined her in the middle of the room, where it had all started. Held her hands, and it was if one thought impinged on both of them, for they stared into each other's eyes, remembering.

He touched the silken hollow at the bottom of her throat. Then touched his lips to hers. 'Shall we go?'

Back home, Shelley was glad she had not stayed the night with Macadam. If she had done so, she was sure somehow news of it would have reached the hospital. The private lives of Barding's doctors and nurses had a remarkable habit of opening up before everybody, no matter how secret the liaisons were kept.

It seemed there was a special gremlin hovering over everybody who was up to

93

something. Shelley had no wish to find herself the subject of whispers behind her back. Bad enough now, with that lively Nurse Little forever fixing her ferret eyes on her whenever Macadam entered the ward.

And was he visiting more often than he was a fortnight ago? She honestly did not know. True, Colum—she straightened lips that were beginning to soften treacherously at the thought of him, resolving always to think of him solely as Macadam—had always been conscientious about his patients. But now, surely he did not need to be so solicitous for Mrs Blaney? She had undergone a vaginal hysterectomy. It had been offered to her as superior to the older method with its ugly abdominal scar. Still young, and with an enviable figure, Mrs Blaney had welcomed anything that would enable her to keep it longer.

'You know what men are like,' she had confided to Shelley when the matter had been discussed. 'There's enough things to set them off their old woman without rotten scars all over the place.'

Shelley agreed. There were too many men who grew away from their wives when something happened to impair their looks. And with so many carefree young girls about without a qualm to their curly heads—it was a thing surgeons knew nothing about. They did what they had to do to a woman's body, and gave little or no thought to what happened when she returned to her family.

Shelley felt better when she had left Mrs Blaney, confident she had built up her outlook. Shelley had met Mr Blaney. Two years younger than his wife, and with a bold eye. She had taken a dislike to him as soon as she had seen him parading into the ward. He did not walk, and there was none of that harried look that surrounded most men when they came to visit their wives or girlfriends. He seemed as if he were expecting admiring looks from all around. The wicked hope insinuated itself into Shelley's mind that Blaney be struck with a vicious case of piles. Maybe that would stop him thinking he was such a gift to women.

She pursed her lips. It was not her job to judge patients' relations. She had enough to do simply to see that Women's Surgical sent their cases on their way, healed, and hoping for continued good health.

She flipped the watch pinned to her dress, and said to Karen Barnwell who had appeared at her side, 'Tea, Staff. There's just time before the rounds start. And we'll need it this morning. Sir Matthew is holding his monthly parade.'

They both smiled, both knowing what a grand tour that would turn out to be. Short by a scant two years of fifty, Sir Matthew was Barding's Grand Old Man of Surgery. A

95

brilliant record, he had built such a reputation that a large part of his time was spent lecturing and on overseas visits.

Shelley liked him, aware of how brilliant he was, and with no off-putting lordly airs. He had made his unstoppable way despite being outside the usual old-boy network. With humble beginnings, his sheer brilliance had been too outstanding for him not to be recommended for ever better posts. There were hospitals in Africa where wards and buildings were named for him. But whenever possible, Barding was always visited once a month. Some said Sir Matthew Conyers loved upstaging surgeons he thought were getting too big for their boots, though every nurse thought he was the kindest, most twinkling-eyed man they had ever known.

Karen sank thankfully on to the spare chair in Shelley's office, and took a grateful sip of the tea Shelley had poured. It was Nurse Little's job to ensure the flower-decorated pot was full at the time Shelley was ready for her morning break. It was on elastic time, but despite her outward look of frivolity, Nurse Little was efficient, and had openly boasted that one day she would be in Shelley's place. Women's Surgical Sister, though not, her eyes flashed impishly, renowned as Sister Immaculate.

'There's oceans of it going on in the world today,' she confided to the more inhibited

Nurse Green, shocking her. 'And I want my share. They called Elizabeth the Virgin Queen, but they won't be calling me the Virgin Sister. Bet on it!'

She popped her head into the office, neat little nose twitching. 'Tea all right, Sister?'

'Very nice, Nurse, thank you,' Shelley told her, blandly impervious to the bright eyes aching to detect everything there was to detect. 'Quite sure everything round the ward is fit for Sir Matthew's eyes? He's an old poppet, but untidy locker-tops give him fits. Make sure Mrs Blaney won't need a bedpan at an awkward time.'

Shelley and Karen exchanged amused looks when Nurse Little's slim figure flashed down the ward, not running, but almost Olympics quick.

'I sometimes think she can read right through to the Marks' labels on my pants,' Karen laughed. 'She's got every bit of gossip round the place tucked up in that cute little head of hers. It will be a relief to us all when she gets married, and out of our lives.'

'She's dedicated herself to being the new Nightingale.' Shelley's lips twitched. In her time as sister, she had been privy to all sorts of ambitions in her nurses—there had even been one saving like mad to make a trip up the Amazon. And had made it. She was now a roving reporter for a national newspaper.

Seeing Karen's disbelieving look, she

added seriously, 'I believe her. I admit that rabbit nose of hers twitches every time she latches on to some fresh gossip, but she is a very good nurse. The patients love her. They love her telling them all about everything—and everybody. Always loading her up with sweets and biscuits. I wonder how she manages to keep that wonderful figure.'

Shelley looked at her watch again. It was restful, talking to Karen. The staff nurse was very close-mouthed about her private life, and Shelley always had the impression it was not over happy. There was the way Karen was so meticulous about leaving on time. Agency nurses were always jealous of overrunning, but in Karen's case it was almost paranoiac.

'I'm worried about Mrs Carey,' Karen blurted out, standing up as she saw her sister was ready to end this time snatched from a busy ward. She went on, 'I went to the doctors' common room yesterday—I was taking a new bleeper to Doctor Marsden—and just happened to catch a few words when Macadam was talking to his registrar. In a hell of a temper—he shut up pretty quick when I knocked—the door was half open—and he saw me waiting there. He was not angry with Mrs Carey, poor thing, but with the way she had neglected having a smear till it was too damned late.'

Shelley felt a little crawl of anxiety round

her shoulders. She still could not help a deep pity for bad prognoses, especially when a case, if it had been taken in time, could have been cured without too much trouble.

'I know,' she murmured, in sympathy with her staff nurse, who was really incensed about Mrs Carey not having a cervical smear test until it was dangerously late. 'It's something that the men who control the money in our profession simply do not take seriously enough. It happens to be a thing men are never troubled with, so they dismiss it as something that can wait at the back of the queue—a long way after new carpets for their offices.'

'Just the same,' Karen said, her eyes blazing, 'something should be done!'

Shelley agreed, but it was less dismaying to talk about the coming Friends of Barding's garden party, to be held in the hospital grounds in a few days.

Shelley had been to them all, since she had been a young nurse riddled with embarrassment at having to dispense tea and cakes to the table of notables, to the present day when she was expected to shepherd prominent visitors to favoured stalls where they could have their pictures taken by Barding's resident photographer, Simon Ross.

He was a theatre staff nurse, whose hobby of photography had made him into such an expert he could have made a good living out of it, but he was welded to his job. Putting human beings together again was far more fascinating than taking pictures of them, but of course, if you were getting married, and were a nurse without too much money, he would gladly take pictures of everybody for little more than expenses.

And as he confessed once to Shelley—after pleading with her to marry somebody, anybody, just so that he could photograph the best-looking nurse in the city—he was so sick of wedding cake and champagne.

'You're going to attend the party, of course, Sister,' Sister Waddel of Women's Medical chortled across the sisters' dining-table in the canteen. Nobody had labelled the long table officially as the sisters' refuge, but nobody not in hospital blues would have dared sit there. Except Sir Matthew Conyers, and he was there today with his favourite Sisters of Mercy as he laughingly called them. Grey-haired at forty-eight, well tanned from his tours abroad, not handsome but distinguished-looking, and frankly wallowing in every item of gossip he could dredge up.

'She certainly is!' he exclaimed, patting Shelley's hand. He had boldly inserted himself next to her, while Sister Grady from Children's had run to the counter to bring him his choice of the dishes of the day. 'I'm expecting her to see I win a prize or two at the fair. They cheat, you know,' he charged, wide-eyed. 'Give you crooked darts for their boards that fly like corkscrews. Give you damned peculiar balls for the coconuts that do all but loop the loop instead of going in a straight line.'

He looked past her to where a tall man was just seating himself at the table where doctors congregated. He pointed without the least qualm.

'Tell me, my dear, who is that young feller? The one with hair like a raven's wing, as you ladies like to call it.'

Over the tables, Shelley caught sight of Macadam still eyeing her as he lowered his plate to the table.

His vestige of a grin bound them as if the two of them were alone in the big room. It was exaggerated thinking, but it felt so true she had a horror of blushing.

'Oh—that's Mr Macadam,' she replied, as calmly as if she knew nothing about him but his name.

'Seen the feller somewhere before,' Sir Matthew said. He poked dubiously at the meat on his plate.

'Gad! If I didn't know better, I'd think it was from a goat.'

He poked around at his food, nibbling, but plainly not enjoying it, trying to act as if he were an unknown young houseman—though

Shelley pitied any clot who made that error.

'Fetch the feller here, Sister,' he commanded, making a try at the Yorkshire. It was the one thing the hospital cook could do well, and it brought a surprised look from Sir Matthew.

'You mean . . . ?'

'Gad! Don't I speak plainly? That black-haired young lad. Fetch him. I know I've seen him somewhere before, and if I don't pin it down it will worry me all day.' His look was suddenly startled. 'Isn't a damn clerk-type, is he? Bumph-filler from Head Office?'

'Oh, no, sir.' Shelley had a job to hide her grin. 'Bumph-filler!' She could imagine the roar that Macadam would let out if anybody called him that. 'He's a very good surgeon.'

'Another cutter?' Sir Matthew's brows rose, then knitted together. 'Gad! Got the feller now! Like a chat with him.' With pretended impatience, 'Well, fetch him. Haven't got all day. Got to get over to Regional Headquarters by three. Damnation pen-pushers. Get rid of the lot of 'em if I had my way.'

Macadam's eyes widened as he saw Shelley making her way purposefully towards him, inevitably pink-cheeked as she thought, 'My sacred aunt! I just know that young ferret eyes is watching. She'll think I'm trying to make a date.'

102

'This is a pleasure, Sister,' Macadam beamed. He rose, to pull out a vacant chair next to him, but she shook her head. 'I've not come to sit here!' she hissed with repressed fury, aware of the ravenous eyes all round the room. 'Sir Matthew's ordered me to fetch you to him. Stat!' she pleaded, feeling the impact of all those eyes.

She turned away, wanting to make it clear she was not actually with Macadam, but he was by her side, his hand on her arm so quickly she could not avoid it.

If he doesn't take his hand away I'll kill him! she vowed. She didn't want everybody to think they were on such intimate terms!

Sir Matthew's bushy brows performed manoeuvres other brows could never hope to reach. 'Sit, young feller,' he graciously accorded. He nodded to a chair just vacated by Sister Grady—who must have been swearing like a docker to herself for not being able to see this enticing little episode through.

'Know you from somewhere.' Sir Matthew pointed his spoon at Macadam, before inserting it into a dubious-looking pudding. He'd encountered worse, he thought philosophically, in his jaunts abroad to this conference or that, he conceded, while his gaze latched on to Macadam like a manacle.

'Munich,' Macadam said easily, not a whit overawed by the summons to the Presence. 'Last year. Very interesting conference on radiation sickness. You were one of the speakers.'

'Was I, indeed,' Sir Matthew grunted. 'Remember the shindig now all right, young feller, but haven't a clue what I said there.' He moved his stocky shoulders, pushed his plate away after one last speculating look.

'Don't suppose I dare light a cigar in this academy to super health,' he chuckled. 'I'll leave it till later.' Ruminatively: 'Gad, I'll need it then. That lot at Regional Headquarters are the most fatuous babblers I've ever met. Bottom-polishers, the lot of them.' Transferring his theme without wasting a second: 'You still cutting people?'

'On and off,' Macadam replied, his quick side-glance at Shelley amused. An imperative nod from Sir Matthew impelled him into a quick resumé of recent cases. His murmured interruption that perhaps the subject was not quite a hit for the lunch-table brought an impatient wave of Sir Matthew's strong-fingered hand. 'All professionals,' he grunted. 'Sides, we've all finished eating, haven't we?' His gaze swept the table. Not a sister felt brave enough to deny the claim, and not one stirred when he added he was not keeping anyone who had work to do. They were not going to miss a second of the time Sir Matthew felt able to spend with them. It was by no means uncommon for him to spray a collection of complimentary tickets for this

104

and that once he was ready to move on. Marvellous seats at the best concerts. Worth waiting for, even if he were the biggest bore to come round the Horn, but even without free tickets he was always good to listen to.

There was a pause, then Sir Matthew glanced at his watch. A cheap and popular make, almost absurd against his elegant suiting. 'Don't let me keep any of you who have to get back to the wards,' he insisted again. He touched Macadam on the arm. 'Have another chat with you at this garden party bash, if you're there.' He glanced round at the entrance. 'I'm waiting for somebody,' he announced. 'Should be here any minute.'

If he expected any general move to the door he was mistaken. And perhaps he knew it, for Shelley was quick to detect the teasing twitch to his lips. He was too grand now to carry out many operations, but he was still well clued-in to hospital ambience, and knew that everybody was waiting to see what sort of person he was waiting for.

It was a show-stopper when she came. She did not just arrive. She made an entrance. Calculated, amusing to her the way she found all eyes swivelling to her as if she had three heads.

Not that she had, of course, just the one, and that superbly crafted by a God who had felt peculiarly elated when he had seen what he had produced.

Perfect features, but lit by a rare animation, as if their owner found life absorbing. Hair like subtle waves of bronze, lighted just as if a stage designer had tried for the effect by the sun that shafted through the corridor window.

She was beautiful, her Paris suit made into a veritable creation by the faultless figure that filled it. Faultless that is, save for one leg, thinner, not obviously misshapen, but far from the standard of the rest of her.

But it was not the leg Macadam was looking at, Shelley realised, while a small thunder went on in her breast. It was the newcomer's face, with that challenging smile curving the poppy-red mouth.

She halted by their table. 'Sir Matthew,' she greeted, and with a pause Shelley thought deliberate, a softly inviting, 'Colum.'

He stood, and only Shelley realised what control he exerted to keep his face a mask of polite attention. 'Eleanor.'

'Colum,' she repeated, the two syllables like caressing hands. 'It's been a long time. Too long.'

CHAPTER SIX

Shelley was grateful for the fact that she was sitting down. If she had been standing, she knew she would have slumped to the floor like a rag-doll. The blood had left her head, so that for a moment, even sitting, she thought she might faint.

Then it was over. She had pinched the inside of her thigh, the sharp pain jerking her back to reality—and to a Colum Macadam who by the looks of him was shatteringly well known to this apparition.

For apparition was all that Shelley could think her. So lovely a girl could have any man she wanted—and from the swift tenderness in her eyes as she advanced on Colum, he was the one.

A piercing humour wrenched at Shelley, forcing her to control the burst of protest that was all too ready to spring from her. At the very moment of her and Colum's meeting on common ground, brought together in spite of their initial antagonism, by discovering in each other exactly what they each wanted, they were wrenched apart by this girl from a past Shelley knew nothing about.

But of course, she told herself bitterly, Colum must have a past. In spite of his harsh, abrasive manner, indeed, because of it, he must have been desired by girls, many girls, even those attached to other men.

A wild hope surged in her—perhaps this girl was already attached. With her looks, and the manner that insisted she was very much a somebody, surely some important personage would have made sure she was his.

She would be perfect for Sir Matthew, Shelley told herself, clinging to straws. Silver-haired, but by no means old. Rich enough for most persons' desires, and in the hospital world, as important as anybody could wish for.

With this girl at his side, they could grace any occasion.

But the hope died as the newcomer reached Macadam, and careless of any opinions around, leaned forward, and kissed him possessively on the mouth. As if, Shelley was stabbed, as if she had kissed that selfsame mouth many times before. They had the look. There was an intimacy covering them that informed everybody they were no strangers to each other.

Macadam rose, and as he ranged himself beside the girl, it was the thing Shelley needed to have her last hope wither and die. They looked so very perfect together. Strikingly handsome, so very sure of themselves.

It was as if Sir Matthew decided that the attention he was so used to as the centre of his little world was being deflected quite enough. Somehow, he was between them. He had an arm round each of them, beaming, eyes alternately on each.

'This is an occasion,' he said expansively. 'And with due apologies to you ladies,' he swept his smile round the table of vastly interested sisters, 'a canteen is hardly the place to greet such old friends as we are.'

He was used to having things his way. The three of them were going to the exit, arriving nurses dividing quickly to either side as if they all recognised royalty when confronted with it, and eventually passed into the cream-painted corridor.

'Well, my dears.' The drily amused, worldly tone embraced them all. It was Sister Melody Clark, tall and quite attractively thin, with a lively face whose best feature was eyes that could quell disorder among patients in Casualty as quick as a police patrol. Never at a loss, never dismayed, she let her bright awareness rest on each of her companions.

'I guess that's just about the Royal Family of this hospital world. Sir Matthew, with more letters and review boards to his credit than you could put in a wheelbarrow, up-and-coming surgeon Colum Macadam— and the famous Eleanor Redding whose last book on neurological disorders is now the definitive text.'

'Those two know each other from somewhere else.' This from another sister, red-faced, hair a little disordered under her stiff white cap. 'See the way they looked at each other!' She chuckled, completely without envy. 'Lord! If only a man had ever looked at me like that! She could have ate him.'

'Well, he is a good-looking hunk,' Sister Out-patients conceded, also without envy. She was a small, deceptively dainty girl, who could keep an eye on several clinics at once, and had a slave-driving manner to young residents and housemen that earned grudging respect. She was young for her job, but she had gathered a harvest of gold medals and certificates in her short career. Discreet rumours said there was a wealthy consultant somewhere in the background, but Sister Allday was sparing enough of information to infuriate her fellows.

She was noticed every time she left the hospital, on her times off, in her green suede suits and gay scarves at her slender throat that made her look like something off a Christmas tree.

Shelley felt encased in a bubble from which she was powerless to escape. She had stopped eating her lunch, and all at once grew aware of a gaze too intent for her comfort from Sister Mullins. From Orthopaedics, she ran her ward with a steely competence that did not make for popularity with either the patients or her nurses. Discontent lodged in her thin features, as if she considered the world owed her—what, she had never disclosed, but apparently it was something Shelley had—or had just lost, judging from the slight curl of satisfaction on the thin lips.

'It certainly looks as if Doctor Redding has her number on our Mack the Knife,' Sister Mullins observed, her gaze on Shelley. It was meant as a goad.

How could she know anything, Shelley asked herself. But then, Barding was a hospital. Gossip clung to everyone—even if it had to be fabricated. It took an effort, but Shelley managed it. 'You must admit, she has style,' she addressed the table. She did not want it to appear she had been challenged by Mullins. 'I dare say most of us would like to be his partner.'

She closed her ears to the drift of talk still audible as she left the table. A murmur of a patient she was anxious about served to get her away without it looking as if she wanted to avoid further skirmishes with Mullins. They would all swop rumours, but would soon change to somebody else. There was never any shortage of names to hack about.

She was almost at her office door when she was intercepted by Karen Barnwell. Karen always looked competent in her whites, but this time, Shelley was struck by how closely she resembled Eleanor Redding. Or was she getting paranoid about the girl!

True, Karen's hair was not quite the burnished red-gold of Eleanor's, but she was similar enough to that ghost from Macadam's past to give Shelley a jolt.

'Something, Staff?' Shelley asked, as

Karen followed her inside the office.

'Just gossip,' Karen replied. Away from the actual work of the ward she had an easy manner with Shelley. Acknowledging her as her technical superior, but letting it be known subtly she was not put down by it.

She stood there, one hand resting on a corner of the desk. 'Is it true there was a visitor in the canteen? A Doctor Redding?'

'Why, yes.' Shelley was surprised. 'Do you know her?'

'I've come across her,' Karen replied. 'I got my SRN at Levington Memorial, where Doctor Redding was in her last year before getting her Fellowship.' Incidentally, her gaze swept past Shelley, apparently on Nurse Rhodes getting Mrs Carey back into bed. Smoothing down the bedclothes with her usual fumble-fisted eagerness, but managing to bring a grateful smile to the woman's worried features. 'That's the hospital where Macadam trained.'

Karen was still unaware it meant anything to Shelley, but she went on, 'They were a hot number.' This time, she did look at Shelley. 'At the time it looked to me they were the closest thing since Dante and Beatrice.'

'They certainly seemed to know each other well,' Shelley admitted. It was an effort—how was it possible she could appear so normal, even manage a slight smile, while holes were being punched in her heart?—but she spoke as if it were all of no moment to her. And if Karen suspected something of what there might be between her and Macadam, at least there was no malice to her conversation, as there was in Mullins' acidic remarks.

'Sir Matthew seemed to know Eleanor Redding well,' Shelley said. 'Or if he didn't, he was taking pains to make it seem so.'

Karen laughed out loud. 'He would. He's lovely with that manner of his. Although,' and her eyes were speculative, 'he isn't really all that old. It's just that his fame seems to have added years to him. He's certainly not too old to be looking for another wife. His first died of an aneurism. I've met him in a couple of places where I've worked, and he's never been far from a pretty face.'

She shut up quickly, as if afraid she was going to reveal too much about herself. Smiled briefly. 'He'd make a fine catch for some ambitious girl. He travels all over the world to this and that big medical bash. And he's got a private income, in addition to what he makes out of his very selective private patients. Nice man, too.'

'Interesting to see how it turns out,' Shelley managed. 'Now, about Mrs Johnson. Tomorrow's her big day. Could you manage a few words with her? I've spoken to her myself, but a bit of extra comfort...'

'Certainly,' Karen assured her. 'Although,' and there was sincere regard in her eyes as she looked at Shelley, 'after you, I don't think I can add any more comfort.' She shook her head. 'Don't damned awful things happen to women.'

Shelley murmured assent, and felt her heart twist again. And more than just surgical needs, she thought. She always knew she would have to pay for her fleeting happiness with Macadam. Nothing in this life was for free. Everything had to be paid for one way or another.

*   *   *

'So you see, there's no other decent way out,' Macadam said to her a day later, reinforcing her view that nothing was free. 'I owe her. She's ready for me to pay her back now.'

'But you said . . . ' Shelley was too troubled to sort out her confusion. Macadam had waited for her as she came off duty. Insisted they had things to talk about.

He had parked his Mercedes a few yards away from the hospital entrance. Nowhere to hinder any traffic in or out of the hospital, but a place where he could not miss Shelley.

And to blazes with any bright-eyed nurses seeing them meet, she thought angrily. But then—did it matter now? There would be no more intimate trips anywhere, no more lovely meals in discreet restaurants, or old-style country pub. Now Eleanor Redding was back in his life, there was an end to all that.

'We were as good as going to be married,' Macadam went over it again, as if repeating it would somehow lift the stubborn resistance she was showing to acceptance of what he had told her. 'We had tickets to the local Philharmonic Hall, Mozart was on the bill, and Eleanor could never resist anything of his, when a car shot across an intersection just as we were driving across. Eleanor was driving. I had just bought a Porsche, and she was mad keen to try it out. This car hit us before she could do a thing about it. Flung us twenty feet into a traffic bollard, and that was it. Eleanor ended with a badly smashed leg, while I escaped with no more than a few scratches.'

He spread his hands. 'It took months before Eleanor's leg was anything like right again. In looks, it isn't too bad, though nothing like as perfect as it was before. But the damage meant she could no longer put a strain on it. Spending hours on her feet operating was out of the question. And she was one of the finest surgeons I have ever known. She had a superb feel for the right thing to do that transcended mere technique. It was as if she felt her way along every vein and ligament and artery, knowing just how to manipulate each. And her neurological speciality . . . ! And it was all over. She tried, but she could no longer stay long enough at the table to tackle anything serious.'

'But I don't understand how you can still feel so obligated,' Shelley ventured. Yet she knew without any more talk. He had made a commitment to Eleanor Redding, and though she had left him for a series of seminars at hospitals and conference centres round the world, using her extensive expertise to teach other surgeons the latest techniques, it had been on the understanding that when she was ready to settle down, she would be back to take him up on his offer of marriage.

'You see—I owe her,' Macadam said simply, his conviction unshakeable. 'If I hadn't been such a damned young show-off, buying that showy Porsche, she would never have wanted to drive it. It would have been me who took the brunt of the crash.'

He raised his hands and slapped them down on the wheel of the Merc, still blaming himself for his youthful macho in wanting a car that was really out of place anywhere but on the autobahns and autostradas of Europe.

'Eleanor's ready to settle down now. That's why she came back. We've kept in touch for the past three years. So...'

So back she comes with her IOU all ready to collect, Shelley's thoughts flashed. For a moment she hated Eleanor Redding. For that beauty that made men ready to wriggle like stupid dogs just for her smallest pleasure, for holding Macadam to a promise made years

116

ago, and which she only now, after she had had her fill of the life she had led, wanted to take up.

She sat there, hands taut in her lap, where she had placed them after evading his attempt to hold them in his. This was no time for such thin comfort. He was leaving her. And no trivial intimacy could change that. Besides, she didn't want him to touch her. Didn't want to face the fact if she found his arms round her, she would immediately forget all about her injured pride, and succumb to sheer need of him. The happiness that had filled her, after they had spent that time together, mocked at her from a memory too overwhelming to keep at bay.

It was a battle to crush that desire for him that tempted her to slip her arm through his, as he sat immobile at the wheel, and hold him as close as she dared. Eleanor Redding had not got him yet. Maybe, if she refused to accept what he had told her . . .

Then cold despair fretted the dim hope that had tried to alter things that could not be altered. Colum Macadam was a complex man, but in one particular, he was extraordinarily simple. He met his obligations. And the most pressing of them now was making up to Eleanor Redding what he considered he owed her.

'I'm hungry,' he said, breaking her moiled struggle with herself. He looked at her, a wry smile plucking at his lips. 'Shall we go somewhere? That place we went to before, somewhere closer to town—or my place?'

His tentative offer of a meal at his bungalow shocked her, showing her once again what she could not have. And how could he even think of food at a time like this! She felt she could never eat again.

Paradoxically, his suggestion pierced her obsession with herself. Made her feel like a wayward child, unwilling to accept the world as it was, stubbornly refusing to face a change that was inevitable.

Her situation now was not much different from those times on the ward when she had to accept the fact that all the nursing and expert care she had devoted to a particular patient were futile. When Death raised a finger, there was nothing to do but wait for the end. It was the same now. Her lips twisted. It would be too theatrical to pretend she was suffering a little death at Macadam's decision. She was just being let down again, although to be fair, this time she could hardly blame him for his loyalty to a previous attachment. And again, he had promised her nothing. It was just that she had anticipated events, and she had nobody to blame but herself. She had wanted him on any terms, and it was no different from those free and easy enticements to buying the good things of life. Buy now, pay later. Well, she was paying, for the later had

118

arrived much sooner than she had expected.

'Now you mention it,' she said, making an effort, 'I do feel hungry.' Making a liar out of herself and her recent decision she could never feel like food again. 'Somewhere quiet. Not too far away.'

She was something nearly herself again. So she could go through the motions of being pleasant. But she knew that at this time, she had better not prolong their meeting. All too soon she knew she would have to be off by herself, hugging herself as if she were a small deserted child, for just long enough to get her disordered world to something like manageable again.

$$\star \qquad \star \qquad \star$$

'Thank God for hospitals!' Shelley murmured to herself next morning, after she had been through the morning report with her staff. There was always too much work to get through to leave much time for introspection. And she blessed her good fortune for having Karen Barnwell for staff nurse. Karen could be left safely to carry on even if Shelley herself was not there. Make a marvellous sister, Shelley thought, regretting once again that the agency nurse's commitments— whatever they were—put paid to any idea of Karen going further in the profession.

'Just the one new admission this morning,

Staff,' Shelley said, closing her book on a fresh entry. 'A Mrs Hendry. Old dear with haemorrhoids. Ordinarily, she would have had to wait for months, but apparently they've become so troublesome her GP finally badgered enough people to get her in. Normally, she'd have gone to Geriatrics, but he also insisted she entered an ordinary ward. It seems she's bright as a button, and was determined she wasn't going to be stuck in with a lot of old girls who didn't rightly know what day it was.'

She met Karen's eyes, and they laughed together. 'Sounds as if we've got a right one here.'

She hesitated, then went on with something that had been itching at her for some time. 'You know, Staff, there's soon to be a lot of new thinking got to be done about Geriatrics. We have all these far-off decisions from pundits who never actually come into contact with the old people I'm thinking of. Men—though mostly women—who arrive at their seventies with all their faculties and as much energy as many people far younger. As far distanced from the old people of earlier times as is modern medicine from leeches and TB care. They may be old in years, and often parts of them may be breaking down, but by and large they are aggravatingly healthy. And getting really angry at being classed as no longer a real part of the human race.' She laughed. 'Take Mrs Thatcher. Can you imagine her accepting the term Geriatric about herself?'

Karen joined in her laugh, but quickly grew serious. 'Me, I just put my head down and do my stint. Never do much thinking about where the nursing profession—or any other profession—is going. Only thing I do know is that everything will have to change soon, or there'll be some pretty sorts of chaos.'

She was halfway to the door when an excited face thrust past her. Nurse Rhodes' plump face was stretched with alarm. 'Sister, come, please!'

She was off, for once her plump form seeming to flit down the ward like her sylph-like fellow nurse, Jo Little.

The other first year was bent over Mrs Baker, in for varicose veins. Slumped awkwardly in the space between her bed and the semi-easy chair beside it.

Shelley found her own heart racing. It had been a while since they'd had a cardiac arrest on the ward, and she had dreaded ever having to deal with another.

'Get the team here!' she shot at Karen, as she hastened to the worried-looking nurse.

Nurse Little was trying to jerk the woman on to the bed, and failing each time. Flustered and hot. Beside the patient, she was a mere wisp of straw. Gladness leapt into her face as she gave way to Shelley.

'Let her lie flat, Nurse,' Shelley said coolly, as she knelt beside them. Then she thumped vigorously on the alarmingly still chest.

'You're not playing pat-a-cake!' she threw out to Nurse Little, without stopping her attempts to pull Mrs Baker round.

'Here!' She reached out a hand, pulled Nurse Rhodes down beside her. 'Keep doing this, Nurse.'

She waited only for Nurse Rhodes to start working on Mrs Baker's chest, before herself beginning mouth to mouth. She registered the fact that Nurse Rhodes had already taken out Mrs Baker's false teeth, and made a mental note to praise the young nurse when the hurly burly died down. They could have choked the helpless woman if they had not been removed.

'Harder, Nurse!' she snapped, in the brief interval snatched to take a breath.

Nurse Rhodes, flushed and unhappy, glared, then flung her resentment into working correctly on the agonisingly still chest.

A clatter of wheels, a stamp of feet, and the red-painted resuscitation trolley swept alongside.

A porter, who had magically been in the vicinity, and experienced enough to lend a hand, grabbed the board always to hand under the trolley, and flung it on the bed. He immediately seized the woman's legs, and with the magically appearing Colum Macadam, heaved the helpless woman on to the bed.

Divining the need, Shelley reached for the indotracheal tube, and manoeuvred it into the woman's mouth, ready for it to be connected.

Macadam nodded approval, somehow infusing a glow of warmth into her, to replace some of the chill stiffness that had so far held her rigid, even though she had gone strictly by the book to bring back the normal sinus rhythm.

'Hundred mils Soda Bic., Sister,' Macadam snapped, not looking away from his patient for a moment. Again that feeling of empathy flashed between them as she wordlessly handed him the already loaded syringe.

She thanked whatever deity looked after nurses for remembering the operations necessary for reviving a cardiac collapse. She had rigged up the drip-stand, to relieve Nurse Rhodes from the make-shift business of holding up the bag with its life-saving drip.

By this time, Azeed Khan, a resident from Paediatrics who had been on his way for a word with a staffer in Women's Medical with whom he envisaged sharing a golden future, had been caught up in the regimented frenzy inevitably surrounding a cardiac arrest, and had readied the discs of the defibrillator machine, and handed them to Macadam.

The surgeon barked for them all to stand back, and held the discs in place for a vital second.

A sigh of helplessness stirred as nothing happened. Mrs Baker's bared chest seemed to mock them with its whiteness, as if wantonly defying them to bring her back to life.

Again Macadam placed the discs. And straightening up, seemed able only to regain half his former stature. But even as another sigh began to breathe unhappily through the group, Mrs Baker seemed to surge up from the bed as if to jeer at them, that she had been playing with them so far, and thought it time to end the charade.

Macadam rapped out an order for the addition of another drug to be added to the drip, further to support and continue the heaven-be-praised resumption of a normal beat to the heart.

Shelley felt the tension leave her as she noted down what had been put through the drip, ready for writing up later, when the crisis was over.

She became aware of the tight grasp of fingers on her arm that held the small pad, and half smiled as she found Sandra Rhodes' eyes on her.

'All over now, Nurse,' Shelley said soothingly, knowing how stiff with fright the first year must be. She had felt the same, the first time she had witnessed a bad cardiac

124

arrest, and she had been a staff nurse then.

Realising how tightly she had been holding on to Shelley for support, Nurse Rhodes gulped. 'Sorry, Sister,' she managed to get out. 'It—it . . . !'

'I know, Nurse.' Shelley patted her shoulder. 'Frightening, isn't it? But you'll be better for seeing how to deal with it. And thanks for doing what was needed. Your progress chart will get a few extra ticks, won't it?'

'Gosh! Never thought of that.' She chased a few happy thoughts through her head, then said brightly, 'Shall I make the tea, Sister?' To herself, she added, 'I'm having one, after that lot!'

'Good idea, Nurse,' Shelley replied, smiling herself now the emergency was over.

Karen Barnwell was in charge of seeing Mrs Baker equipped with a new nightie, the old one ripped unceremoniously from her by Macadam when he arrived on the scene.

He was standing beside Shelley now, surveying the efficient way Karen was helping the orderly to move Mrs Baker from the ward. She would be going to the ICU for the rest of the day, for closer observation than would be possible in the general ward.

If she were to have another attack, it would show immediately on the battery of monitors in the ICU, where an experienced nurse was always on hand.

All at once, Shelley felt ill at ease. Macadam was watching the scene lose its tight-strung air of harassment, and assume its orderly routine. If he was aware of every eye and ear cocked towards him, as he stood there with Sister, he gave no sign. He knew of course, of the frenetic urge to become part of every bit of drama in a ward that all the patients had. They did not want anything bad to happen to any of them, but something like what had just happened made the boredom of hospital life disappear for a short time. It made them feel important themselves, like those old beldames of the French Revolution, who knitted at the guillotine, imagining that they themselves had had a hand in the committee that had sentenced these popinjay aristos to the relentless Madame.

'I imagine there'll be tea ... ' ventured Shelley, wanting desperately to escape the focus of every eye around her. It had never bothered her before, she thought wrily, but Macadam had altered her world. That world had been so tidy and secure, where as Sister Immaculate she had reigned with a supreme confidence that had held her inmost feelings inviolate.

Was there an even more curious gleam in Nurse Little's eyes as she scurried past with a covered bedpan for the agonised-looking woman in an end bed who had apparently decided that now there was no more drama

126

she could attend to a more personal problem?

'Tea!' The stiffness wiped from Macadam's face. Nobody in hospital life could survive a cardiac arrest without feeling a battle had been fought. The effects could not be dismissed immediately. 'Good idea.' He glanced at the expensive Rolex on his wrist. 'Got time, fortunately, Sister. These battles with that old fellow with the scythe do leave one wrung out, don't they?'

It was an admission of human weakness that surprised Shelley. Macadam had seemed so rock-like, so impervious to the more human emotions. But it warmed her to him, and she was glad that it had been Macadam who had been so close to the scene when the cardiac arrest alarm had been sounded. They had worked so closely together—she recalled those few glances during the first desperate moments when he had acknowledged her help, and felt a stronger feeling wash through her.

And sitting there in her office, on a corner of her desk, one leg in its elegant saxony suiting swinging idly as he sipped his tea from a large mug that Nurse Rhodes—sturdy as a small oak herself—had thought more suitable for a big man than the thin cups Sister herself favoured, he all at once assumed an extra highly Technicolored image that made Shelley lower her head. It was only by a great effort she could control her face, stop herself from revealing herself like a Dayglo poster.

Why did the sight of him so relaxed make her thoughts fly to sunlit beaches, topless, and peopless! Topless, because deep within her she was proud and exhilarated by knowing she would decorate any beach—and she craved his admiration as a woman, not the chill merit he awarded her as Sister Immaculate, whose ward favoured perfection.

'Have you thought any more of going to Japan?' she asked, sweeping her mind away from sunlit beaches in case she betrayed herself.

'Thought, but it will need a lot more of the same before anything concrete results,' Macadam replied. He looked away, down the ward where Nurse Little was in a strategic position to see them both—not that she was actually spying, but they made such a spine-titillating topic when she was at her cronies' table in the canteen.

'I've a lot of work to do before anything can be really considered,' he went on, his gaze somehow seeming to retreat into other interests. 'I've a backlog of private patients to sort out. And I can't simply leave here, just like that. It all takes time. And of course, there's . . .'

'Eleanor?' Shelley asked. He could never know what effort it cost her to utter the name so idly, as if nothing about that radiant personality was important.

'She's keen to come with me,' Macadam said. His gaze was still fixed on something that did not seem to include Shelley Vyner. Certainly, not those sunlit beaches that had so engrossed her a few moments before. Unless it was a beach where the bathers were all toothy Japanese, except for the two Occidentals—one of whom was unmistakably Eleanor Redding.

CHAPTER SEVEN

It was not usual for a sister to accompany a patient down to the theatre for an operation. Normally, Shelley would not have considered it. Not that she thought herself too important for such a job, but because it was a useful way for young nurses to find out just how much most patients dreaded going to that large room where those powerful lights hovered like menacing beacons.

The gowned staff, doctors and nurses, were all hushed in solemn ceremony apart from the subdued symphony of steel instruments making their clinks as they were lifted from their steaming baths in the small room next to the theatre. Everything contributed to a high drama wherein every patient occupied far too important a part.

Mrs Crest particularly. The night before,

prior to going off duty, Shelley had stopped by her bed, and in the seclusion of the drawn curtains, spoke quietly to Mrs Crest. She mentioned how the woman had benefited from the small rest since she had entered the ward, before she was scheduled to go for her operation. The frightened look from the hazel eyes increased, only retreating a little as Shelley took the hand straying restlessly over the green-spotted coverlet.

Shelley let the human touch work its small comfort, then said, 'It isn't really as bad as you fear. You won't know what's going on, and before you know it, it will all be over. You'll be back here. Another short while and you will hardly remember you were ever in here. And you will know you have been saved a lot of grief.'

It was not the words, commonplace as Shelley knew them to be. The sort of syrup doled out too often as a palliative to frightened people. But there was nothing else to say. It was the very evident concern and encouragement in Shelley's face, the slight pressure she put on Mrs Crest's hand, that produced the required effect. A statement that Mrs Crest was not alone, about to be marooned on an operating table with nobody caring very much. There would be doctors and nurses shepherding her through the whole thing, all wanting her to recover and go back to her family.

'I know I shouldn't be frightened,' Mrs Crest said, apologising for putting another burden on this sister who seemed to understand so well—and her really too young to be a sister—though everybody said she was something special, that no nurse ever frowned or hesitated a moment when she made one of her soft voiced requests. 'It's just that it's so—' she faltered for meaning '—such a woman's thing that men don't...'

Her words trailed away, but Shelley did know. She had seen women like this come into Barding far too many times lately, with the same complaint, something that could have been treated as a very minor thing if action had been taken when the cancer first reared its ugly head. She hoped fervently that Mrs Crest had not left it too late.

'If you could come down to the operating room with me,' the trembly voice went on. 'I know you're so busy, but I'd feel—if you were there...'

'Of course.' Shelley squeezed the hand that still lay in her grasp. 'Night Sister will give you something to make sure you have a good sleep, and I'll see you again in the morning.'

So it was not unexpected she would find Macadam just leaving the theatre and almost bumping into her where she had just left Mrs Crest on her trolley, to wait for the anaesthetist to take her in charge.

'Morning, Sister.' Macadam stopped his

131

half-charge towards the small office where Theatre Sister always had a pot of tea waiting, for Macadam liked a cup between each operation, even at the cost of a fresh scrub.

'Funny place to find you,' Macadam continued, his gaze sharp under the green theatre cap.

'Mrs Crest,' Shelley said simply, gratified to find instant comprehension in his face. How could she ever have thought him merely a dextrous Mack the Knife, slick with the cutters, with no more feeling for what he was doing than a fishmonger filleting a plaice?

He scowled, manoeuvred Shelley into the office, motioned to the pot. Now she was here, she could help. She had to hide the flood of feeling that rushed through her in the simple act of pouring him out a cup of tea. It seemed to bind them in a way that no words could express—until she remembered . . . !

'The sort of thing that makes me furious!' Macadam said, between sips. 'Makes me wonder at the priorities in the NHS. The way money is poured into glamour operations, heart-lung transplants et al., while we get miserably cheese-paring over seemingly trivial things like making sure breast cancer clinics are set up. Enough tests at the right time and we could save surgeons' time and many lives.'

His eyes bored into her. 'I know heart-lung transplants are fine, but it's only one person. Think of the money involved being turned to something that could save hundreds of lives of women who are so vitally needed by their families.'

'Mrs Crest was so frightened,' Shelley interrupted. If Macadam's views were heard by the wrong person it could damage him. The boys of the glamour operations boasted a very strong lobby. Barding itself was hoping to set up a super-facility to carry out these complicated operations. The fact that such a complex would inevitably drain the hospital of nurses and ancillary staff from every more ordinary ward would be brushed aside, except by those nurses who would find themselves even more overworked.

'I'll do the best I can.' Macadam nodded, showing he thought he had already dallied too long. Still, his gaze lingered on her, as if he wanted to tell her something.

It came out like a bullet. 'Seems like Eleanor's made up her mind.' In the doorway, he paused, for a moment bleak as winter. 'I owe her,' he said bluntly. Then he was gone.

Somehow, Shelley found herself on the way back to her ward, back to the sanctuary of her office, where, with an array of forms and cards in front of her, she could make believe she was working instead of trying to still the tumult of protest and anger that stormed through her.

To be fair, she could not honestly blame

Eleanor Redding. Her career as a brilliant surgeon had been halted. But she would not be the only doctor who had been forced to change courses in mid-stream. There were plenty of other openings in the medical world where she could make her mark. But she had dallied, kept Colum on a hook, then when it suited her, come back into his life to make him fulfil the promise he had made her when he had been feeling guilty. It was just not fair! Even now, she was leaving Colum, still hung up, because it suited her purpose, by going off on a world tour with Sir Matthew, before returning to the cake and orange blossom.

True, the tour was business. She would be a big help to Sir Matthew. At conferences, hospital visits, be a ready companion when he met important people in his world. But at night there would be the after-ski business, light-hearted and enjoyable at first-class hotels, their expenses-paid trip like winning the New York State lottery.

Shelley raised her head, looked out into the ward. Everything so ordinary, peaceful. And here she was, sitting here with her well schooled face, making sure nobody, most of all lynx-eyed Nurse Little, would seek out what devastation had been wrought in her life.

Colum and Eleanor would be married, and they would go off to Japan. By the time Sir Matthew had finished his ego-boosting journey, Colum would have finished his short contract at Barding, and would be ready to take off on his own trip abroad. Along with Eleanor. Together they would travel through Japan when it was at its best, in cherry-blossom time. Trips to sacred Fujiyama. The mad blur of Tokyo, and the special squads they had for cramming more passengers into the already crammed trains. And the backward little fishing villages where they could watch the dawn come gilding the sky as the bobbing fishing-boats spread their sails and lifted to the breeze that would push them out for another day's work.

Shelley had run the Technicolor journey through her mind a dozen times, thinking of a new marvel each time that she simply must visit, and now it was all gone, a magnificent film she would never see.

Never walk across those funny little bridges into those wonderful tea-gardens, with Colum's arm round her waist. She tended to dismiss the visits he would have to make to various hospitals, the collection of facts and photographs for his proposed treatise, but in their way, they would be just as interesting—and she would be helping him. She was already embarked on a course of shorthand, in case he wanted her to take notes.

She smiled tightly. Well, the shorthand might come in handy, if she decided on a change of career herself, and opted for the administrative side of the NHS, instead of being fastened to a surgical ward. They were always on the watch for fully experienced sisters who wanted to leave the dirty-hands side.

The light tap on her door brought her head round. In the doorway, a buxom girl with raven hair smiled at her with none of the diffidence that might be expected, even in these less regimented hospital days, usual from a lesser light. Immaculate white dress, blue belt, but with much more forwardness than generally expected from an SEN.

'Morning, Sister,' Connie Fallon greeted. 'I've been told you're short-handed, so here I am.'

Her manner was like a dawn breeze, refreshing, invigorating. She was an Irish nurse who had been well trained in getting along with difficult people by five brothers, and still revelling in a room of her own in the nurses' home. No desire to go higher than a blue belt, but with an uncanny knack with patients that made her much sought-after.

Shelley felt her depression lift. She had used Connie once before for a stopgap, and would have gladly hung on to her if she had been able.

'Good morning, Nurse.' Shelley got up. 'Shorthanded is something we always are, but today, it's even worse. My staffer hasn't come in. She phoned in sick an hour ago.'

'Even nurses can get ill,' Connie smiled. 'Now, where would you like me to start, Sister?'

'The drug round,' Shelley said gladly. She had been expecting to have to do it herself, not quite trusting her young staff. There were so many drugs with long names these days—how simple it was when Black Draught and Mist Aper Alb figured importantly in the daily dosage, and today's drugs had to be administered with scrupulous accuracy.

Connie waved a hand. 'It's done, Sister.' She beamed. 'Am I glad I got moved here. I've been in Geriatrics the last fortnight. Lovely old things, most of them, but sweet Mary Mother of God, they do depress the life out of me, though sure and it's no fault of their own.' She shivered. 'Hope I die before I get like that.'

She accompanied Shelley to the drug cupboard, accepted the key, and ran through the drugs for each patient, carefully checking the location of each patient. Happy-go-lucky she might be, but in hospital work, she was as good as anybody Shelley had ever had.

And she made a difference to the atmosphere in the ward. She was friendly with all the women inside the first half-hour, lifted the mood of her fellow nurses, and indeed, of Shelley herself.

It came as an unwelcome finish to the day

when Shelley realised it was her evening at the battered wives' hostel. After her few words with Macadam that morning, she would gladly have skipped it. But she had promised her friend, and knew how much Millicent depended on her, not so much for the work at the place, but for the uplift that Shelley's visits gave her.

'I can be sure you'll be one person who does not turn up here with a lumpy face and black eyes all over,' Millicent laughed ruefully. 'It gets you down here sometimes, so you forget there are ordinary people in the world out there. People who don't get thumped regularly, just to keep them nicely trained.'

Millicent's manner grew swiftly businesslike. 'Got two new arrivals.' She took the coffee container off the hotplate—it was always there ready, and to blazes with taking in too much caffeine. They didn't have to run a battered wives' hostel, those wiseacres.

'Little scared piece. Enough bruises to stuff a pillow, and two loose teeth.' She glared at Shelley, taut and angry. 'Think there'd be any chance of a law authorising wives to carry knives for self-protection?'

'They would never use them,' Shelley said. 'Too many of your victims tend to welcome the beatings. At least it assures them they are not being neglected.'

'Ha! Not my idea of care and comfort from

138

a loved one!' Millicent snapped. 'The other new one's a bit of a mystery. Won't give any name, or particulars. Just needs a place to stay for a few days till she makes some arrangements. Ready to make a donation, and you know, we are always hungry for money.' Thoughtfully: 'A much better type than usual. Weird.'

Shelley finished her coffee, washed her beaker at the small sink. 'I'll look in on your regulars,' she announced. 'Maybe the reticent one will open up to me.'

The slender figure, hunched over slightly in a well worn armchair in the lounge where the wives gathered to watch TV, looked instantly familiar. But it was the tawny hair with its vigorous wave that stamped the identity of the new girl on her awareness.

As if Shelley's immediate halt in the doorway tugged at the girl's attention, she turned her head. Made to speak, but nothing emerged from her dropped-open mouth.

Karen Barnwell jumped up, breaking through the shock that gripped Shelley. She stood aside as Karen came to the door, let her through, then followed her to the end of the passage. Karen faced her with a strangely defiant air, mixed with a resignation that found Shelley wanting to put her arms round the girl. She had never seen Karen so beaten. She had always been so capable, forthright, able to cope with anything. And so very insistent always on keeping her private life private.

She stood now, one shoulder pressed against the wall, figure a little slumped, as if it were an effort to sustain the well got-together look that had always characterised her.

And there was no use pretending, her semi-defiance seemed to say, that there was no huge bruise round her right eye.

'I guess it's no use telling you I walked into a door?' She still tried to cling to shreds of defiance as if it were the only thing left holding her together.

The astonishment at finding Karen here had ebbed from Shelley. She had had time to read the misery and hopelessness behind the front. It was desperately clear Karen wanted to talk. There were things bottled up in her that must have been lurking there all the time—or at least a lot of the time—she had been working at Barding.

But this was not the place, Shelley thought. She took Karen by the arm, widened her eyes as Karen winced.

'Not all of it shows,' Karen admitted ruefully. She made no more comment while Shelley took her into the office.

A ball-point pen stuck in her hair that made her look like an overlarge pixie, Millicent took in the scene with instant comprehension. She pushed aside the heap of papers she had been studying, sighed, and

140

kicked back her chair. The legs bore the marks of many such kickings, as if Millicent had swung away from her desk many times bristling with indignation. An indignation that loosened a little as she made a gesture as if to say the place was theirs.

'Got a few things to see to,' she murmured as she passed Shelley in the doorway. 'Plenty of coffee, or' she waved to a cupboard behind the desk, 'brandy. Medicinal only.' Her grin was companionable, indicating many of the wives coming here had dire need.

Shelley found biscuits, delaying the whole thing a little, to give Karen time to assemble what she was going to say—or not say. Finding her ward sister here, Shelley thought, must have been a real blow. It was one thing to seek a hiding-place where everybody had troubles, but quite another to find an acquaintance there, somebody who would want to know so many things hitherto kept secret.

Shelley recalled the way Karen had shrunk from her when she had taken her by the arm. How long had the abuse been going on? Usually, battered wives sought refuge only after a long period of abuse.

'I'm sorry you have to find out,' Karen said hesitantly. 'I never had any inkling when I thought of this place. I'd heard about it from one of our patients who had a friend ... ' Almost in exasperation: 'I never expected to find a sister from Barding here. And you certainly are not a battered wife.'

'I come every Tuesday night, unless something keeps me away,' Shelley explained. 'I know it is not the sort of place you would expect to find a colleague, or you would never have come. But Millicent is an old school-friend. When she found the money to set this place up, she asked me to look in sometimes to give her moral support. And of course, there was generally a bit of first aid for me, and then, most of the women seemed glad to unburden to me. Millicent herself is a strong character, too abrupt sometimes to encourage confidence, so she is grateful for every bit of help she can get.'

She let Karen finish her coffee, poured her another. 'You can tell me or not,' she said carefully. 'There are all sorts of reasons for men hitting their wives on a regular basis, and I don't suppose your tale is much different from dozens I've listened to. The only thing that is my business, is your work at Barding. I realise you won't want to appear on the ward with that eye, but when you feel like coming back . . .'

'I'll have to hand in my notice,' Karen said crisply. Her head was high. She was not going to continue as a battered wife, that was clear. 'I've a friend in Kendal. We both used to rock climb a bit, before we got married. I can board with her for a time, until I get fixed up with a job and a new place of my own. Greg and I are finished.

Defiant, definite. She looked at Shelley, as if waiting for questions. None came. Shelley just waited. It would come.

'It wasn't always like this,' Karen began, her words coming with a rush, as if held in too long and now had to boil out. 'We had a lovely home. A good life, if a shade too outgoing for me. But Greg insisted he had to keep up a life-style suitable for a rising young executive. He worked for Allday Plastics. Medium-sized, fairly new outfit, and very progressive. Greg was Sales Director, a real whiz-kid. Looking forward to becoming Managing Director after a few more years. Then—they were taken over.'

It all became clear. Shelley had had friends, before arriving at Barding, who had gone through the same experience.

And Merkle International was a large conglomerate. Dozens of companies. They had enough of their own whiz-kids. Super-sharp young men hardened in all the techniques of bringing new firms into the fold, and shaping them to the efficient cost-productive mould that was Merkle.

Karen shook her head slowly, as if she still did not really understand. 'Greg was out. Merkle did not need any more whiz-kids. And Greg was no longer so young. From looking forward to a bigger job, joying in his own Porsche instead of the company's sedate Sierra, he found himself, to be cruel, just another statistic in the dole queue.'

She shrugged. 'He tried. Thought a man of his calibre would find something very quickly Got listed by headhunting firms, management lists, but—nothing. He started to drink. He'd always liked it socially, and he began to need it. I had to go back to work. But only agency nursing. Not like you and the others, what I call real nurses. Greg wanted me home every night, on the dot. To get his tea. To look after him. To talk to. Then that wasn't enough. He wanted somebody to blame. I was there. I was it.'

She tried to laugh. 'You must have heard this scenario a hundred times. At first it was just a few knocks. With a joky laugh. Nothing really much. And he was always careful not to mark me, so the neighbours would know. But it began to boil up really bad. Over the weekend he got into a rage.' She pointed to her eye. 'It went on and on, and this was the result. But no more. I'm not going through any more of it, because it will only get worse.'

'Will you be coming back to Barding at all?' There was nothing else for Shelley to say. Her expression showed all the sympathy Karen wanted. Shelley was businesslike, the efficient ward sister, the sane prop Karen needed.

144

'Just for a week or so, while I get my arrangements made with my friend. And a few other bits of business to see to. I'll find myself a place while I wind up at Barding, then...'

'You can have my spare room,' Shelley found herself saying. She valued her privacy. Had valued it ever since she had moved out of the always crowded nurses' home. But behind the sane way Karen was responding she sensed a hurt so deep it would eventually leave a lasting trauma, if some help were not offered.

Karen's head rose. Surprise, reluctance, then gratitude, shaped her features.

'I'd like that,' she said simply. 'I'll be here for another couple of days. I'll join you at the end of the week. I'll phone. And by next Monday, my face ought to be presentable enough so I can get by with the old ran-into-a-door bit.'

*　　　*　　　*

When Shelley closed the door of her flat behind her, she leaned back against it, not really happy about having her home invaded, even for the short time Karen expected to be there. Shelley had come to value her own place, where she could be just herself, without need to shape her behaviour or thoughts to anybody else. It helped her step

145

away from the multitudes of traumas that were a constant in Women's Surgical. Where she could drop for a time the mask of super-efficient Sister. Where she could kick a cushion if she felt inclined, without wondering if lynx-eyed Nurse Little were around.

In the event, Karen Barnwell was quite a welcome guest. Underneath her everyday always pleasant behaviour, Shelley sensed a sadness that her life had been damaged, but a determination nonetheless to go through with her decision.

It matched the sadness Shelley herself could not escape, about Colum Macadam's decision to carry out his pledge to Eleanor. Shelley could admire his integrity, and though she wished sometimes he were otherwise, she knew that if he had been any different, she would not have loved him so much.

But it was difficult to remain unmoved when every time she stopped by Mrs Crest's bed, the woman sang Macadam's praises. The fright had gone from her. 'Yes, I am sore, in places,' she almost blushed. 'But I do feel a lot better. I feel as if I'd just escaped a terrible worry. I can't tell you how it feels, and how grateful I am that your Mr Macadam talked me into having the operation. If he hadn't been so—so nice, I would never have come in.'

'Nice!' Shelley smiled as she helped Mrs Crest to a more comfortable position. Nice was hardly the word to describe Macadam. Not with that rocklike jaw. But he did have moments. She could feel a rippling pleasure touch her nerve-ends, could almost see his face in front of her, the way it had looked when—when . . .'

She snapped back to her patient, managing to disengage herself before another paean of praise rang in her ears. All that was gone, for ever. And all she had left was a memory of what might have been, if Eleanor Redding had not come back into Macadam's life.

Cherry-blossom time in Japan! She could save, and perhaps manage a trip in another couple of years. She winced. Why waste the time when Colum would not be with her? And winced again when she thought that perhaps, if she somehow made the trip, she might run into him if he were still there—him and Eleanor!

She swung round, pausing only to speak sharply to Nurse Rhodes about the state of the sluice, before seeking the sanctuary of her office.

She did not see the hurt looks that passed between Nurse Rhodes and Nurse Fallon. A tinge of amusement in the more tolerant Irish girl's eyes.

'Ah, don't take on so,' Nurse Fallon's soft Irish voice urged. 'Even an angel has a black monkey on her back now and again. Come along now, and I'll give you a hand before those stuck-up doctors have their morning parade.'

★   ★   ★

It was a relieved Karen Barnwell who settled into Shelley's flat—only as a temporary measure Karen insisted. 'You're damned good to put me up at all. I hope we can still stay friends. I would hate to damage our relationship.'

'Well . . . ' Shelley turned away from the phone which had rung almost as soon as she had entered. 'Your eye's practically better,' she said abstractedly to Karen, her mind busy with the totally unexpected phone message.

'Thank heaven for that!' Karen said feelingly. 'I hated being away from Barding. I never thought I would miss the place so much.' She raised her hands in mock despair at Fate. 'I guess a nurse away from her proper job always feels like a piece of flotsam.'

'You'll be all right, here on your own?' Shelley asked, as if Karen had not spoken. She was still wrapped up in the call from a neighbour of her Aunt Myrna. Juggling train times, assessing the possible chaos her absence from Barding would cause. The PNO would grant her immediate leave. That was beyond question. And after all, Shelley

148

thought philosophically, nobody was indispensable.

'My aunt has had a heart attack,' Shelley said, mentally going over the situation again. She would have to leave Karen here on her own, but then, Karen was a level-headed girl, and there was no likelihood of her having a carouse in the flat with her husband—not after the thin-lipped declaration she had made about being finished with him for good. She could suffer anything, bar infidelity or physical violence. That final black eye had set the seal on months of hurtful indignities.

'There's a chance I'll be gone by the time you get back,' Karen said, as she watched Shelley snap her case shut. 'I've been in touch with my friend. Just a few things to settle here, and I'll be off.' She put a hand on Shelley's arm, almost out of character, for Karen was not a demonstrative girl. Capricorns were not like that, she had said more than once. 'I want to thank you for being such an angel.' Her lips twisted admiringly. 'But then, what else can I expect from Sister Immaculate.'

Shelley winced. 'God! That label! I'll never live it down. I'm just as human as anybody else.'

'Better organised,' Karen said softly. 'Well, arivederci, as they say in Rome. I hope your aunt is over the worst.' Just in time she suppressed an impulse to say, 'It must be hell

149

to lose your only living relative.'

For that was Myrna Freshfield. Nothing like her namesake, the pert-nosed star of the thirties cinema. Named after the star, but never anything like her. Thin as a rail, severe-faced, but well conditioned to laugh at herself and her foibles, with an old-fashioned rectitude, but tolerant about others, that betrayed itself in many acts of kindness for her neighbours and friends.

It was one of these, a homely body by the name of Mrs Ricketts, who lived in the bungalow next door, in the small seaside town where Myrna Freshfield finally planted her roots, who echoed Shelley's heart-felt relief at finding the heart attack nothing more than a muscular spasm. But a definite warning.

'Frightened me out of my wits,' Mrs Ricketts admitted, able now to laugh at her distress on finding her friend sprawled apparently lifeless in a chair. 'First thing I did after calling an ambulance was to call you.' It was not criticism in her eyes as she looked at Shelley. 'I knew you would want to be here. She thinks the world of you.' Smiling: 'Probably never let you guess it, but she's nowhere near as uncaring as she likes people to think.'

'She took me over when I was sixteen,' Shelley reminisced aloud. 'You don't need to tell me about Aunt Myrna. And I'm glad you called me.' Guiltily: 'I should come up here more often, but you know how things go . . .'

'I know,' Mrs Ricketts said sadly. 'My own children always have so many things they have to do before they can manage a visit, but that's the way it works. We're never as important to our children as they are to us.'

Shelley found her aunt already rebelling at hospital strictures. Looking as tough and weathered as the timbers of the fishing-boats she loved to watch coming in with their catches.

'I'm signing myself out tomorrow,' she declared defiantly. 'The very idea! Me taking up a bed needed by somebody else. I can rest just as well at home.'

Nor was she any more palliative when she did go home. Refused Shelley's impulse to remain longer. Her niece was a nurse, Myrna insisted, and heaven knows, there were never enough of those. She had better take herself back to where she was wanted, not hovering around here where she was beginning to make her aunt feel she really needed a nurse.

So Shelley found herself returning a few days sooner than she had expected. And relievedly. For once the anxiety over her aunt had ended, she could not keep her thoughts from Macadam. Every moment she was not engaged on something that demanded all her attention, she found herself thinking of his strongly resolute face. She berated herself for acting like a lovesick teenager, but could find no reasonable answer to the proposition that surely a grown woman could be as confounded by love for someone as much as a girl ten years younger. There were no age limits to love.

It was as if a puckish whim of God had brought them together at a time when Shelley felt woefully travel-weary, dragged down by her long journey, and aching for a shower.

She was stepping away from the cab that had brought her from the station to find Macadam at her elbow. In a glance, she took in his almost gaunt face. The intense brightness of his gaze as it examined every part of her—leaving her infuriatingly aware of how bedraggled she must look.

He took the case from her hand. She was still in shock at seeing the object of so much heart-burning in front of her, like an answer to prayer—or, remembering his decision about Eleanor, a nightmare.

'You've been away!' He rapped it out as if she had set out deliberately to bother him. 'I've been away myself for a few days,' he went on, belligerently as if she were the cause of a whole lot of inconveniences. 'I thought you'd be at work today.'

'I had to visit my aunt in Humberside,' she said. She let him into the house, preceded him up to her flat. Keyed open the door, and stood aside to let him enter with her case.

She was unbuttoning the mac that the

expression in his eyes said so beautifully moulded a figure worthy of a glossy magazine cover, when the door of the spare bedroom opened.

Shock ripped Shelley's so brief euphoria into ribbons. A man was halted in the doorway of the room she had allotted to Karen. Once handsome, now puffy-eyed, slack-jawed, scowling at them as if they were unwelcome intruders.

Beside Shelley, the case Macadam had carried into the room dropped with a thud. She half turned, saw outrage, contempt, and incredible bitterness crowding his shocked face.

Just as Shelley had glimpsed the man's half-naked form, dressed only in red striped shorts, Macadam had taken in his apparent living-in look.

For one moment, agonised, Macadam had stared at Shelley. Tightened his lips to stop whatever his mind was making of the situation from emerging, then turned on his heel, and stormed out. His heels beat an explosive tattoo to the front door.

Shelley swallowed. She could hardly find words. What she wanted to do was strike this—this oaf, across his bleary face. Beat him to a pulp.

'Who the devil are you?' she managed at last.

CHAPTER EIGHT

For a lingering moment Shelley thought it might be all a dream. That this puffy-faced man in his disgusting undress, with an undeniable scent of whisky blearing from him, would vanish.

But he stood there, swaying a little, his eyes narrowing, as if trying to fit her into his life. He held onto the edge of the door to steady himself.

'You must be that bloody sister she's always talking about!' he said disagreeably. 'That paragon!'

Before Shelley could find words to tell him she realised who he must be, the outer door opened. Breathless, Karen Barnwell rushed in, her face falling into horrified lines as she confronted the two of them.

'Oh, Greg!' It was a half-wail, a half-scream of forlorn despair. All the agony of a destroyed relationship was on her as she took quick steps, pushed him with all her strength into the bedroom. 'Get yourself dressed, you object!' she hissed.

She slammed the door on him, still holding on to the knob as she faced Shelley.

'God! I'm sorry!' she breathed, distress a clamp on her. 'I would not have had this happen for the world.'

Shelley, her own world in ruins, recognised another soul in distress. After the sight of Macadam's infuriated face, nothing could be worse. 'I just didn't expect you to invite him here while I was away,' she said tiredly.

'Oh, Shelley—please!' Her eyes begged Shelley's pity. 'It's not like that at all! I didn't invite him. I wouldn't dream of abusing your hospitality like that. He followed me here. Pushed himself in, and was so damned drunk I couldn't get rid of him. He just slumped to the floor and snored like a pig.'

As Shelley still remained silent, what with still remembering the look on Macadam's face unable at the moment to take in the scene with her usual cool competence, Karen explained.

'While you've been away, I've been coming back here for lunch. I could use the phone without interruption, to call those people I wanted to know what was happening.' Hurriedly, 'I've put enough cash aside to pay for the calls. Then today, Greg must have been watching the hospital, and trailed me here. Pushed in the minute I opened the door, and promptly went out like a light.'

She faltered then, bitingly aware of Shelley's rigid stare. 'I just dragged him into the spare room, put a pillow under his head and left him on the floor. I couldn't lift him on to the bed, nor did I want him on it. He must have woken up, undressed, and probably crawled into bed to be more comfortable.'

She let her words trail into a confused silence. Tried to drag a smile from her tumbled emotions. 'I suppose Greg heard you come in, and thought it was me. I would never have let the devil stay here at all, but he was legless.' She gestured helplessly. 'I didn't expect you back for another week. You would never have known anything about it. Still, no real damage done.'

'No,' Shelley said listlessly. No damage. Only whatever had brought Macadam here unknown, and probably never would be known after this. His spontaneous rage said clearly enough she had a live-in lover. The idea of getting Macadam to listen to her explanation almost made her burst out in idiotic laughter.

He knew nothing about Karen staying here. How could she ever hope to have him believe the truth. He would only look at her with even more contempt, and storm off in that hurricane fashion that had already left her so shattered.

And now, she would have to face him every day. So close to him, as he told her of what he wanted done. So close—and yet a million miles apart!

Something inside her seemed to wrench her apart. Of course, she would not, could not, go on like that. She would not put up with such antagonism every time their work brought them into contact.

Somehow, she survived the muted drama of Karen getting her husband away. And the almost immediate departure of Karen herself, from Barding. Now she would be able to get down to the business of whether to leave Barding herself, or whether there was some way she could sensibly continue there, waiting until Macadam went off to Japan.

She could stand his withdrawal from her. Put up with his chill manner, that eliminated her from the list of persons he wanted to admit to his small circle of intimates. Heartbreak! She smiled twistedly. There was no such thing. Real discomfort, truly. Loss of appetite, loss of sleep, a troubled mind. They could all be borne, knowing that in time there would be an end to it.

Reconciled to a period as unhappy as her first heartbreak, over that smooth-tongued young resident who had introduced her to the endless sagas of Romeo doctors and all too eager young nurses, she woke one morning with a sense of disaster.

Her worry over her continuing relations with Macadam suddenly were eclipsed by something really meriting worry. She realised she had missed her period.

Under the stress of Karen Barnwell's untimely intrusion into her life, she had allowed that usually simple matter to slip her mind.

Sitting on the edge of the bed, finally awake enough really to appreciate her position, Shelley ran a whole gamut of emotions and ridiculous plans through her mind. It all ended in a shaky laugh as she turned off the shower—comfortable now in body, if not in mind. In her time as sister, she had listened sympathetically to several wide-eyed, halting confessions from nurses who sensed in her a comfort and source of immediate help they badly needed.

How many times, when they had left her office, reassured at least that somebody was there to help them, had she mentally shaken her head, wondering why women never learned. A few words from a silken tongue, a temporary surge of passion—and a life perhaps totally upset. In fact, it had happened so often that Shelley had adopted the habit of giving any new girl on her ward a few words of advice, concerning the beguiling ways of young doctors.

And now here she was, caught in the same biological trap, as if she had been as careless and witless as any seventeen-year-old let loose the first time from the strings of a cautious mother.

As she dressed, putting on the sister's new blues she had brought only the week before, Shelley closed her mind on a decision. She thrust aside all objections. She had never really envisaged leaving Barding—unless being whisked away by some fascinating doctor—but somehow, before Macadam appeared there had been no real chance.

She forced her attention away from the thought of him in Japan, with a beautiful and understandably excited Eleanor Redding beside him, breathlessly eager to plunge into all the delights Shelley had conjured for herself.

Fate had a ruthless way of thrusting a finger into the affairs of mortals, destroying plans and hopes and ambitions. It had destroyed hers. And all that remained was to pick up the pieces and start afresh. Fortunately, Shelley smiled at herself thinly in the mirror, she already had a very plausible excuse.

Aunt Myrna, God bless her! Hale and hearty again after her brief scare, but the PNO was not to know that. Shelley restrained herself from painting her aunt as a pathetic creature, able to manage only if Shelley were there all the time. Caring for her.

Rhea Bryce sat at her desk, not very large in her discreet navy blue with a frill of white at the throat that gave her a Madonna-look with no hint of the iron will behind those cornflower-blue eyes.

She set her pen down neatly beside the single sheet of paper—she was famous for her neatly written statements of what she wanted done in her sphere of operations, which she presented at regular intervals to the hospital's committee of management, resumés that were always carefully examined. Rhea was as difficult as a handful of hot potatoes if she did not get her suggested improvements.

'This is a surprise, my dear,' she said gently, not probing, but behind her sympathetic gaze a world of conjecture. Like so many others, she had come to regard her Sister Immaculate as a fixture at Barding. To lose her . . .

'My aunt is not young any more,' Shelley interposed. 'When I spent those few days with her recently, I was surprised at how much she had gone down.' She shut her mind to the uproar her Aunt Myrna would have raised at hearing that. 'She used to be so vigorous. Fortunately, it was not a real heart attack, just a muscle spasm. Nevertheless, the doctor warned me, out of her hearing. She needs somebody with her.'

As Rhea Bryce sat silent, already moving and adjusting the personnel at her command in her mind, Shelley went on, 'I owe her such a lot, Ma'am. When I was a child, she took me over. What I am, she had a large part in.'

'And an excellent business she made of it,' Rhea Bryce commended. 'I would like to meet her—in different circumstances she would probably have made as good a sister as you have done.'

She did not speak for a few moments, sipping the tea her secretary had brought in. Watching Shelley drink hers. And without making it obvious, she caught a hint of the strain behind her favourite sister's carefully schooled face.

It couldn't be, of course, Rhea Bryce told herself. Her Sister Immaculate had always been so reticent about any relations she might have had with the male medical staff of the hospital. So discreet. But then, she was a woman, and a very beautiful one. And there had been just the slightest whisper—that thrusting new surgeon, Macadam—over whom she knew several of her young nurses had lost their heads, and would willingly have lost other things if he had given them the slightest encouragement.

'Well,' she spoke, there was never enough time to spend on the welfare of every nurse who appeared in her office, and she was due at another wretched committee meeting, in which nothing concrete would be resolved, just more talk from people who seemed to have nothing else to do but talk. 'If you must leave us, Sister, then you must. But I part with you with great reluctance. I had thought, if I could have dragged you away from your patients, that at some time, this office...'

She rose, signifying the interview was over, but somehow, still reluctant to have Shelley leave.

'If it is at all possible, I would like you to return to Barding. I like to think we are good enough to be staffed by the best nurses in the North. Sisters especially. They are a race apart. Laughed at so many times as bloodless spinsters with their funny little ways. Tolerated generally, respected mostly, sometimes even liked. Once in a while they inspire the devotion of all the nurses they work with. I have them come to me, Sister Vyner, asking to be put on your ward. I cannot give a greater accolade.'

She held up her hand. 'Goodbye, my dear. If ever I can help you...'

Somehow, Shelley got out of there, past the secretary, and outside. There she went past the glowering face of the head maintenance man, who was waiting for a talking to. He was reinforced and bound by union rules, but he still failed to relish a stinging interview with a woman as decisive and plain spoken as Rhea Bryce.

Shelley told nobody she was leaving. If she had allowed the news to escape, there would have been endless interruptions in her work, people trying to get to know too much, curiosity rampant, maybe even jolly get-together on her last day. Something went to ice inside her. She could not tolerate that. The good wishes, the curious looks—and if they only knew. Knew how she dreaded keeping on until the truth grew obvious. She could imagine the hands up to faces, hiding the sniggers, the looks from eye to eye, the acid comments of some of the sisters who had always envied her speedy accession to blues, and especially her looks.

Sister Immaculate indeed! It just goes to show!

She blessed Rhea Bryce's warm-heartedness, so well hidden behind her razor-sharp manner. It enabled her to get away from Barding at the weekend without the formality of three months' notice. Shelley felt a little ashamed at using her aunt as a subterfuge—and when she thought of it, almost certain the PNO had guessed the reason for her quick departure.

She did not have the heart to cut her links with Barding in any dragged-out manner. She simply packed a few things, phoned her aunt, and took the first available train. Thankful for the few passengers so that she would not be disturbed too much, preferring to let her thoughts pick a miserable way through a life changed so drastically in the last two weeks.

If only ... She braced herself against the seat-back, firming her lips. She did not regret that passionate time with Macadam. She loved him—and knew that when it had happened, he loved her. Perhaps he still did. The possibility warmed her, started a thin hope, till she crushed it with the

163

purposefulness of somebody facing an uncertain future that was going to be totally different from the one she had expected.

Macadam had made his decision. Had felt bound by his promise to Eleanor Redding, so that now she had finally made up her mind, she would not expect him to desert her.

It was a disaster, but at least she had got away from Barding without having to undergo a time of curious eyes and furtive whispers.

Aunt Myrna was not one for hugging. Never had been. She put one arm round Shelley as she stood on the doorstep, pulled her close, and dropped a swift kiss on her cheek.

'You've solved my problem for me,' she greeted Shelley matter-of-factly, as if Shelley had just arrived from work. 'I was tempted by two splendid pork chops this morning, and didn't know whether to have one fried with onions today, and the other casseroled tomorrow with whatever happens to be in the larder. But now you're here, I'll cook them with mandarin oranges, make a sauce from the juice. Mrs Ricketts gave me the recipe, and I've been waiting a chance to try it. But cooking for one does restrict one so much.'

By this time they were in the comfortable living-room, kept spare of unnecessary furniture, so moving around was no problem.

It had never entered Shelley's mind not to

tell her aunt why she had so suddenly decided to uproot herself. She knew her aunt never asked questions. She had her life, Shelley had hers. If Shelley wanted to tell her things, she would listen, offer advice, and all the help she could.

The pork chops, tender as pride, flanked by crisp French beans, appeared in no time. Preceded by a touch of brandy Aunt Myrna insisted was strictly medicinal, that loosened Shelley's hold on herself. It was a relief to spill it all, a relief to have her aunt survey her with that never-blaming look of hers, so shrewd, so sturdy.

'Don't you think you should have waited a bit?' she asked. 'You know how these things can be.'

Shelley gave a wry smile. 'The real thing that made me determined to leave Barding was I couldn't any longer face Colum—Macadam—every day. To think of him going to marry Eleanor Redding—it was just too much. Thinking I might be pregnant only provided the spur.'

'What do you mean—thinking you were pregnant?' her aunt asked, brows raised. 'I thought . . .'

Shelley grimaced. 'So did I. But it was a false alarm. After such a long abstinence, I guess my biological clock got upset. I started again this morning. But I'm still glad I left. I couldn't stay there.'

'So, what are you going to do now?' Aunt Myrna was never vague. 'Not right this minute, of course. But when you've had time to get used to our sea air.' She paused. 'Only too glad to have you. But there isn't much going on here, not for a girl. I love it, but it is quiet.'

'There's a hospital within a few miles,' Shelley replied. 'Charnbury General. Only been up five years. Takes in everybody from what they call a catchment area of about a hundred square miles. I should imagine they have room for a sister about the place. I'll write them, then just wait.'

'Good,' Myrna approved, ever practical. 'We might as well use you while you're here. We'll decorate your room. Have it all done in a day if we keep at it. Monday, we'll go into Charnbury. There's a very good bus service fortunately. Choose some paper, paint, what we need.'

It was marvellous therapy, Shelley thought, as they finally put away their brushes, and folded the paste-table to stow away in the small shed at the rear of the house. Half the time she had been able to forget Colum Macadam. Forget that so brief flaring ecstasy of their time together. Forget the plans they had made in the euphoric aftermath, when she realised she loved him with a deep and enduring love. She was almost sorry now that there was no child to arrive. It would have

166

made a break in her life, but with her aunt to help, she could resume her ordinary way soon, and Colum's child, something of his . . .

It was just breakfast-time the next day, when Myrna presented herself, already dressed for departure, holding one of the hats she liked to wear on her short, greying hair.

Funny, Shelley thought, smiling up at her aunt. Myrna's hair always seemed to have been that colour, really neither one thing nor the other, so very different from her decisive manner. Nor did she seem to age at all. Even her recent scare had done nothing to shade the look of robust good health about her.

'Going somewhere?' Shelley asked. She was already dressed herself, though it was barely seven o'clock. She had never been the dressing-gown type. If you're up, you're up, she used to say. If you're up, you should get dressed. Perhaps that look of always shining readiness at the break of day had contributed to her being called Sister Immaculate. Perhaps it was from her aunt she had caught the habit, for Myrna never lingered herself over the toast and marmalade, with crumbs dropping on to a dressing-gown.

'School governors' meeting,' Myrna said briefly. 'Pour me another cup, dear. I've had my breakfast, but it will be some time before I get another cup of tea.'

'Aren't you early for a governors' meeting?' Shelley asked drily.

'Things to do before then,' her aunt said. 'I'm looking in on a friend of mine when I get to Charnbury. Rina and I enjoy shopping together.' She waved her hand. 'Days for the governors' meetings I always cram in as many other things as I can.'

'You should get yourself a Mini,' Shelley advised. She relished the toast made from the bread her aunt bought. It still tasted like bread.

'And what will you do with yourself today?' Myrna paused in the doorway, her smart black pouch-bag under her arm. 'If you feel energetic, there are always the cupboards.'

'Oh, heavens, not cupboards!' Shelley groaned. 'The one thing about hospitals I've always hated. So many cupboards, and so many of them forever in need of tidying. Those and the sluice!'

Myrna pecked her cheek. She believed in a swift kiss, never prolonged. Anything more tended to be sloppy, and she hated that. Perhaps that was why she had never married, she pondered sometimes. Was it unnatural to dislike people touching her? But there it was, and she had reconciled herself to it.

'You'd better get yourself back into a hospital soon, dear,' she advised. 'You're looking quite lost already.' A brief nod, full of unspoken affection, for Shelley was looking down at the table, and could not see the giveaway emotion. 'Well, 'bye for now.'

The door closed behind her, with the crisp snap typical of all her aunt's motions. Everything so decisive. No shilly-shallying. Shelley laughed softly. She pitied the other governors. They could beat against her aunt's steadfastness of opinions as uselessly as the sea so close at hand beat eternally against the two grim headlands that looked so very menacing but provided a safe harbour for the small fishing-fleet.

Shelley's face brightened. She would later stroll along to the quay where the boats tied up. It was a long stone finger, jutting out into the harbour, providing a safe anchorage for the boats, and with sturdy posts where the men could drape their nets for mending. A place for gossip, if the walnut-visaged men felt like speaking. Sometimes they did, sometimes they did not. Shelley had long ago solved the equation of speech or no speech by considering the catches the boats brought back. Although, as she soon discovered when she paused by the first little group of men discussing their hauls, even here things had changed.

'Not like it used to be, not any more.' That was Danny Furlow, an incredibly young sixty-five, and with as much thought of retiring as of jumping into the sea he sailed over so often.

'Sea's changing,' he vouchsafed grimly, putting his stubby pipe back into his mouth as if that explained everything.

'Aye, 'tis that,' Tom Cawson backed him up. His twinkling eyes proclaimed he was just as ready to chat to this very engaging young female as Danny Furlow, and had a better claim, since he knew her aunt quite well.

'Have to go further out now before the water begins to look like water.' He stopped suddenly, to rephrase something he had been about to say, which would scarcely be suitable for his listener. 'So much oil-spillage these days, lazy skippers washing out their tanks hardly a stone's throw from shore, and the Lord knows what muck washing into the sea from factories and power-stations. There'll be a day when all the fish must up and die.

'Maybe not in my lifetime, but it will surely come. And there's many a fish we have to throw back again nowadays. Too horrible looking even for scampi.'

He guffawed. 'Scampi! God, I'd sooner eat a mud turtle!'

A man who had not spoken so far, about her own height, with a calm peace about him that made Shelley warm to him, said suddenly, 'And how's your aunt, Miss?'

She was startled. Somehow, even though her house was so near to this quay that was a natural meeting-place for the locals, she had never envisaged her aunt having anything to do with these men.

'You know her?'

'Sort of. She's a rare busy woman these days. Tell her Fred was asking.'

He said no more, but murmured something about getting back, wherever that was.

There was a winding path that started beyond the straggle of houses at the end of the village. It bore upward, beyond bushes and straggly gorse that bent grudgingly to the stiffish breeze that was always there, as much a part of the scene as the sturdy headlands that embraced the harbour.

Shelley breathed in happily. The sun was out, spreading its warmth everywhere, seeming to add whiteness to the spread gulls' wings as the birds lifted easily over her, before swooping down towards the water of the bay.

It was idyllic. Peaceful. And it bored her to death. Before, when she had come here to stay, she had enjoyed the peacefulness after the bustle of the hospital. But now, she missed the busy ward. Felt as if she had somehow been cut adrift because she was not returning there. It was that which made the difference. Then, she had been a somebody. Now, she was a nobody with nowhere to go. And even if she found a place at Charnbury General, it would never be the same. That was the trouble with putting down roots, leaving an awful cut-off feeling when they were severed.

And worst of all, abandoned by Colum

Macadam. Not that she could, in fairness, call it being abandoned. He had presented his decision to her, hating it like she did, but impelled by that promise he had made to Eleanor. She thought of Colum, and found her eyes blearing with tears. It hurt to be with him, working so close to him, and knowing he belonged to someone else.

Yet now it hurt so much more because she was so far from him, and could not see him at all. Never see again that treacherous little twitch of his lips when he was going to smile. Not that he smiled overmuch—she hated a too easy smile—but when it came, especially for her, there was such joy in it.

She brushed a hand fretfully across her eyes. And again, damning herself for being such a fool as to think him actually there, conjured up into a mocking spectre that almost assumed reality.

She had thought of him so often, dreamed up his image, only to have it fade so quickly, sneering at her inability to put him out of her life forever. As he had so successfully done with her.

She shook her head. Damn him! This was worse than it had ever been. It must be the quietness here, no sound but the distant wash of sea so far below and the shriek and wail of the ever-circling gulls, that had made the object of her thoughts linger more than usual.

'Well, pearl of my dreams, aren't you even

going to say "Hello?"'

She scrambled to her feet, shocked, disbelieving. Yet a hammering exaltation threatened to make her sink to the ground again.

'Mr Macadam—Colum!' She could say no more. She knew the blood was seeping from her face. Her knees grew so weak she swayed, and was grateful for the strong arm that swept round her.

She looked into his eyes. The softness there, the yearning, burned into her. When his other arm went round her, she pressed against him, terrified he would vanish, a figment of her dreamy state after all.

Then his mouth descended on hers, firm, demanding, its bruising effect rousing her to press harder against him, so that finally he had to release her, to stand apart a little, still with his arms round her, signifying that from now on that was where they were going to remain.

'Mr Macadam!' she breathed.

'Don't you think you could stick to Colum, now we are going to be married?' he teased.

'M-married! But ... You said ...!'

'Come,' he said gently, easing her to the sun-warmed grass. 'We have things to talk about, so we might as well be comfortable. Out of the wind here.'

Shelley felt light-headed. She did not care about being comfortable. She would have

173

been just as joyous, just as thrillingly caught up, if they had been sitting in a draughty shed in Siberia. Colum had come back. He had come for her—and was going to stay with her. Commitment was in his face stamped there so indelibly, words did not matter.

She moved her mouth away from his, but made no effort to wriggle away from the arm that held her so closely. She had wanted it there so often, and so often despaired of its ever being there. Now it was. She did not need explanations. Not yet. Later she could listen to them. For now, she was content to enjoy the wonderful bliss that enclosed her, savour again the love that firmed his lips on hers, his hand on her breast, not demanding, just emphasising his possession of her.

It was Colum himself who wanted to explain. He had had such an agonising time since he had discovered Shelley had left Barding. Spent so much time finding out where she had gone, finally bearding Rhea Bryce in her office, insisting if she knew an address where Shelley had gone, she must give him the information.

She had studied him coolly, enjoying his uneasiness. She did not have a cruel bone in her body, but she remembered the tight-held control that had kept Shelley's raw nerves from destroying her when she had sat in this office, insisting she had to leave.

'So—you're the one,' Rhea Bryce said

softly.

The steadiness of her gaze bothered Macadam. He had heard the PNO was a tough nut—he had not forgotten the soft voiced demand she had made of him some time before at Shelley's insistence he curb his enthusiasm for operations—and now he realised her reputation was merited.

'The one what?' he said as pleasantly as impatience allowed.

'The one who persuaded my favourite sister to leave. I did not believe for one minute that her aunt was so bad Shelley had to go to look after her. I knew there was a man somewhere in it.'

In his turn, Madadam studied her. 'All right,' he admitted tightly. 'If Shelley did leave here because of a man, I'm it. Do you know where she is? With this aunt?'

'Yes.' She let the silence build, waited till she sensed he was near breaking-point. She had not had much to do with Macadam. He had not been at Barding long enough for her to get to know him well. But she thought he had a much shorter fuse than the suave consultants who formed the elder statesmen of the hospital's hierarchy.

'Did I hear you were going to Japan when your present contract ends? You took up a rather short one, didn't you?'

'I did. It filled in the time before I was ready to go East. I'm committed to go to

175

Japan. And Shelley Vyner will be going with me if you can only tell me where I can find her.'

She laughed then, a softly musical sound given to few men to hear. 'I think you will have your hands full,' she told him. 'She isn't quite the Madonna she looks. But then, you will probably be good for each other.'

'If we ever get to meet again,' Macadam said shortly. 'I can lay my hands on some scopolamine quite easily, you know.'

'That won't be necessary.' She informed him of the small village on the east coast where Shelley had gone. Halted him in the doorway. 'Good luck, Mr Macadam.'

'But then, I don't need luck, do I, my precious?' he murmured, turning Shelley in his arms so he could reach her lips more easily.

'No—but perhaps you need a good story,' Shelley taxed him. 'Last I heard, you were only waiting for Eleanor to finish her grand tour with Sir Matthew to rush along to the nearest bishop for a special licence. And then heigh ho for the slopes of Fujiyama. What happened?'

'You happened,' he said. 'Once I found you had left Barding, I felt as if I had lost my very life. I knew no matter what I had promised Eleanor, I couldn't go through with it.'

He laughed grimly. 'I sweated over a whole

weekend, trying to think of the best way to call it off—and the very first thing she said to me when she arrived back in town, after her tour with Sir Matthew was "I'm sorry, darling, but I can't marry you. Sir Matthew..."'

'You mean ... ?' Shelley could not finish.

He nodded. 'Sir Matthew happened, too. He carries a special sort of charisma where some women are concerned. And travelling with him, from one important engagement to another, Eleanor all at once found she had far more in common with him and his life-style than she would have with a much less important medic who still had his way to make in the world of medicine. They were married yesterday. Eleanor very kindly let me off the promise I had made to her—and very relieved I didn't kick up a fuss about being gazumped.'

He smiled wrily. 'Apparently, one trip to Japan on limited expenses would nowhere near make up for a continual round of important conferences all round the world. If you care for that sort of thing. Apparently Sir Matthew has a golden key.'

Shelley felt an overwhelming gladness pulse through her. She was almost delirious with happiness. She had made up her mind soon after meeting Colum for the first time that he was the only man for her. And now here he was—and they were wasting time talking about two people who did not matter a button to them.

'You still mean to go to Japan, then?'

'Never more determined. My contract with Barding ends at the year end. It will give us nice time to make arrangements, time to reach our destination, and for me to make a start on the research I want to do—and give you time to set up home for us.'

'In one of those lovely little houses with sliding doors and mats to sleep on?' Shelley prompted.

'I think perhaps something a little more to the taste of Europeans,' he said. 'Though perhaps for the ceremony of Taralaba we will rent a typical Japanese house, sliding doors and all. For a month or two. In the summer.'

'Taralaba?' Shelley was mystified. 'Is it something . . .'

'A festival of lovers,' he breathed gently, hand on her breast as if to inform her as lovers they were a perfect choice. 'It comes once a year, in July. Provided it does not rain. A pair of stars, Vega and Altair, are honoured by the festival. The lovers are supposed to exchange poems. An old Japanese custom.'

'Poems? You mean we're supposed to write them ourselves?' She could not take her eyes off his face. It was not especially handsome. Distinguished, rather, and anyway, she did not really like handsome men. She preferred a touch of ruggedness, and the man looking so intently at her was somebody she would enjoy looking at for the rest of her life. She rested her hands on his shoulders, joying in the possession of him.

'I can't write a poem,' she ventured shyly. It was barely possible to move her lips, so eagerly did he want to possess them.

'Not true,' he murmured, brushing butterfly kisses all over her face, ending on her eyelids. 'Can you think of a finer poem written anywhere than the simple words "I love you"?'

Photoset, printed and bound in Great Britain by REDWOOD PRESS LIMITED, Melksham, Wiltshire